"You're Being Very Contradictory Tonight, Samantha. They'd Eat You Alive In The Boardroom With That Attitude," He Mocked.

She stiffened. "Listen, Blake, I'll sleep with any man I want when I'm good and ready. Tonight I just wasn't ready. And in case you didn't notice, this isn't the boardroom."

No, but he did want to eat her alive right now.

Adrenaline pumping through him, he knew it was time to take action.

"Blake?" she croaked as he brought her into the circle of his arms, leaving only sheer inches between them. He'd never been this close to her before. Not close enough to see the rush of desire in her blue eyes. It knocked the breath from his body.

As hard as it was, he let her go. He knew all he needed to know for the moment. She wanted him. And he wasn't giving up. His plans for seduction were still very much alive.

Dear Reader,

I was thrilled when my editor invited me to write the fourth book in the Dynasties: The Jarrods series. Better yet that the setting was Aspen, Colorado. What a gorgeous place for my hero and heroine to fall in love.

Being a writer is like being an actor who needs to get into character, and that made it such fun to write this book. I especially enjoyed writing a heroine who decides she has nothing to lose by instigating a brief affair with her handsome boss before she walks away forever. Samantha turned into such a tease. As for my hero, Blake didn't know what hit him. He'd been forced to return home to take charge of the luxurious resort, determined to remain indifferent to the place and the people. He hadn't counted on the majestic mountains, renewed family ties and the love of a beautiful woman like Samantha to show him what really mattered most.

Like the beautiful Colorado scenery, I hope Samantha and Blake's love story takes your breath away.

Happy reading!

Maxine

MAXINE SULLIVAN

TAMING HER BILLIONAIRE BOSS

Published by Silhouette Books

America's Publisher of Contemporary Romance

With thanks to the fabulous Silhouette Desire editors,
Krista Stroever and Charles Griemsman,
who worked so hard to make this series special.

And to friend and Harlequin American author C.C. Coburn
for her helpful advice on everything Aspen.

Special thanks and acknowledgment
to Maxine Sullivan for her contribution to the
Dynasties: The Jarrods miniseries.

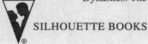 SILHOUETTE BOOKS

ISBN-13: 978-0-373-73055-1

TAMING HER BILLIONAIRE BOSS

Recycling programs
for this product may
not exist in your area.

Books by Maxine Sullivan

Silhouette Desire

The Millionaire's Seductive Revenge #1782
The Tycoon's Blackmailed Mistress #1800
The Executive's Vengeful Seduction #1818
Mistress & a Million Dollars #1855
The CEO Takes a Wife #1883
The C.O.O. Must Marry #1926
Valente's Baby #1949
His Ring, Her Baby #2008
High-Society Secret Baby #2021
Taming Her Billionaire Boss #2042

*Australian Millionaires

MAXINE SULLIVAN

The *USA TODAY* bestselling author credits her mother for her lifelong love of romance novels, so it was a natural extension for Maxine to want to write her own romances. She thinks there's nothing better than being a writer and is thrilled to be one of the few Australians to write for the Silhouette Desire line.

Maxine lives in Melbourne, Australia, but over the years has traveled to New Zealand, the U.K. and the U.S.A. In her own backyard, her husband's job ensured they saw the diversity of the countryside, from the tropics to the Outback, country towns to the cities. She is married to Geoff, who has proven his hero status many times over the years. They have two handsome sons and an assortment of much-loved, previously abandoned animals.

Maxine would love to hear from you. She can be contacted through her Web site at www.maxinesullivan.com.

From the Last Will and Testament of Don Jarrod

…and to my beloved son **Blake,** I leave the grand piano that was your mother's pride and joy. Some of my fondest memories are of you, lying beneath that piano, listening to your mother play. I hope you will find room in your home for this beautiful piece and enjoy not just the beautiful music it puts forth, but the true love it represents.

One

"What are you doing in here?"

Samantha Thompson almost dropped her pen as her head snapped up, the desk lamp shedding enough light for her to see the handsome man standing in the doorway. "Blake, you scared me!"

Her heart didn't settle down once she knew who it was, it only increased pace as she looked at him in a dinner suit that fitted his well-toned body flawlessly. His commanding presence was of a man born to lead. This was Blake Jarrod, owner of Blake Jarrod Enterprises' Las Vegas hotels, and now the new CEO of Jarrod Ridge, his family's renowned resort in Aspen, Colorado.

And as his assistant of two years there was nothing unusual about her being in his office at ten at night. Just because they were now in Aspen at the Jarrod Manor and she was using the desk in his late father's office didn't change a thing. She had her reasons for being here.

And they concerned her boss.

Or soon-to-be-ex boss.

"It's late," he said, cutting across her thoughts in the way he usually did.

She took a steadying breath and looked down at the letter in front of her, giving herself one last chance to change her mind. Then she remembered this evening. The final straw had been watching a famous blonde actress flirt outrageously with Blake, and him sitting there enjoying it, taking it as his due.

Samantha couldn't blame him for wanting to sample what was on offer if he so chose. It was just that *she* wanted a little taste of him herself. She usually dressed sedately in finely tailored clothes whether she was in Vegas with Blake or here in Aspen, but tonight she'd outdone herself. She'd worn this slinky cream evening dress designed to grab his attention, putting her long, brunette hair up in a chignon when she usually wore it pulled back at the nape with a barrette, but it was clear now that nothing was going to happen between her and Blake.

It was *never* going to happen.

She'd realized that when he'd caught her eye and she'd smiled for all she was worth, looked the best she could be, and he'd turned back to the actress without a second glance, rejecting her just like Carl had rejected her. Her moment of epiphany had been that simple. She'd come to a decision then. The right decision for her. The *only* one for her.

She lifted her gaze. "Yes, it's late, Blake."

Too late.

He walked toward the desk, almost as if he sensed

something wasn't quite right. "I thought you said you were going back to Pine Lodge."

That had been her intention. She'd even stood in the lobby of the manor, her coat resting on her shoulders, waiting beside the doorman for the valet to bring the SUV around. She'd been determined to go back to their private lodge at the resort—she in her own room and Blake in the master suite.

Then someone had entered the hotel and the doors had slid open, and the cold night breeze from a midfall wind had slapped her in the face and chilled her to the bone, reminding her that it didn't matter what she wore or what she did, her boss would never take any notice of her except as his assistant. She'd spun around and headed for the private elevator, coming up here to the office in the family section of the manor.

"I needed to do something first," she said now.

There was an alert look to his eyes. "It's Friday night. Work can wait until tomorrow."

They'd been working every Saturday, trying to keep on top of things until they moved here permanently. And now that wasn't going to happen. Not for her anyway. "This can't wait."

He paused, those blue eyes narrowing in on her. "What can't?"

She swallowed hard. "My resignation."

Shock flashed in his eyes then went out like it had never been. "What are you talking about?" he said, his voice quiet. In control. He was *always* in control, especially where she was concerned.

"It's time for me to move on, Blake. That's all."

"Why?"

The question shot at her like a pellet but she managed to shrug. "It just is."

He put his hands on the desk and leaned toward her. "What's this about, Samantha? What's the real reason you want to leave?"

She'd faced him down over business issues occasionally but this...*this* was personal. Cautiously, she pushed the leather chair back and rose on her stilettos, then went to look out the large arched window behind her.

The scene below at the luxurious resort was surprisingly charming in October. Tonight, pocketed in amongst the tall peaks, the sleepy hamlet twinkled like fairy lights in the alpine breeze, a tapestry of winding streets, lodges, and village square. To a southern California girl who now lived in Vegas, this place had something nowhere else seemed to have.

It had heart.

"It's time for me to go," she said, keeping her back to him.

"You're unhappy here?"

"No!" she blurted out, swinging around, then winced inwardly, knowing she sounded contradictory and that he'd have to wonder why.

To be truthful, she'd been feeling slightly down ever since Blake's sister Melissa had announced her pregnancy a few weeks ago. She'd been happy for Melissa, so why it had bothered her she didn't know. Yet since then she hadn't been able to shake a feeling of being slightly depressed.

He'd straightened away from the desk. "So what's the problem?"

You are.

I want you to notice me.

Dammit, I just want *you*.

But how did you say that to a man who didn't even notice you as a woman? She was his trusted assistant and that was about it. She'd never acted overtly female around him. She kept everything businesslike between them. Looking back, perhaps occasionally she should have let her feminine side show. If she had, then perhaps now she might not be in this predicament.

Yet it wasn't that she was in love with him either. She was intensely attracted to him. He was an exciting, charismatic man who effortlessly charmed women like they were going out of fashion, but he was still discerning in whom he took to his bed.

She wanted to be charmed by him.

She wanted to be in his bed and in his arms.

Oh, God, it truly was hitting home that she'd never be in his spotlight. Until now a glimmer of hope had kept her going, but after his subconscious rejection of her tonight, she'd realized that if he knew her feelings about wanting him, then everything would change. She'd be totally embarrassed and so would he. She couldn't work like that. She'd be humiliated just like she'd been with Carl. It was better to leave with some dignity.

"Samantha?"

Hearing her name on his lips struck her like never before. She tilted her head at him. "Do you know something, Blake? You've never called me Sam. Not once. It's always Samantha."

His brows drew together. "What's that got to do with it?"

Everything.

She wanted to be Sam once in a while. Sam the

woman who'd left her ordinary upbringing in Pasadena to embrace the excitement of Vegas after a one-sided love affair gone wrong. The woman who wanted to have a purely physical affair with a man she admired, without ever risking her heart again. Not Samantha the personal assistant who helped run his office and his life and who kept the whole lot in check for him, all nice and neat and tidy, just the way he liked it. She couldn't believe she'd actually thought she'd had a chance with him.

And he was waiting for an answer.

"I have my reasons for resigning and I think that's all you need to know."

"Is someone giving you a hard time?" he asked sharply. "Someone from my family? I'll talk to them if they are. Tell me."

She shook her head. "Your family's great. It's…" She hesitated, wishing she'd given herself time to come up with a suitable explanation. Needless to say, she hadn't expected to be here tonight writing out her resignation, or that he'd even come upon her. She'd assumed he'd probably go off nightclubbing with Miss Hollywood. "I simply want something more, okay? It's nothing against you or your family. This is about me."

One eyebrow rose. "You want something *more* than first-class travel and a world-class place to live?"

"Yes." She had to tread carefully. "Actually I'm thinking of going home to Pasadena for a little while," she fibbed, then realized that wasn't such a bad idea after all. "Just until I decide what I want to do next."

"And that will give you more of what you want? I seem to remember you saying you'd left Pasadena *because* you'd been looking for more excitement."

She'd definitely said that—and she *had* been looking

for more than weekly piano lessons and weekend shopping with her girlfriends—but it had been so much more four years ago. Having fallen in love with a young architect who'd gone off to travel the world after she'd told him she loved him, she'd decided to find her own excitement. Her job with Blake had provided that excitement without any emotional involvement. Until now. And even now it was about lust, not love.

His eyes pierced the distance between them. "You seemed happy enough before to move to Aspen."

"I was… I am… I mean…" Oh, heck. She was getting herself tied up in knots. When Blake said he was moving back home and she should come with him, she'd been delighted. His estranged father's will had stated all the Jarrod offspring had to return to Jarrod Ridge for a year or lose their inheritance. Blake, being the eldest—only by a few minutes ahead of his fraternal and more laidback twin, Guy—had taken up the challenge of running the resort.

She'd looked forward to it, too, and they'd been traveling back and forth between Aspen and Vegas a couple of times these past four months, getting everything sorted. Blake would keep his hotels but would spend most of his time in Aspen. She'd been very happy with that. Until tonight.

She cleared her throat. "All my family and friends are back in Pasadena. I miss them."

"I didn't know you *had* any friends."

She pulled a face. "Thanks very much."

There was a flicker of impatience. "You know what I mean. You're always working or traveling with me and rarely go home except for the holidays. Your friends have never been a priority before."

"I guess that's changed." Thankfully Carl had never returned and she'd heard he'd married an English girl. Of course, time and distance had only shown her that she hadn't really been in love with him at all. She'd been in love with the *idea* of being in love with a man who'd talked of adventure in far-off places. She'd thought they'd do that together. God, what was wrong with her that she kept wanting men who *didn't* want her?

He held her gaze. "What are you going to do after Pasadena, then?"

"I'm not sure. I'll find something. Perhaps even one of those rare friends of mine might help me get a job," she mocked. All she knew was that she wouldn't continue working for Blake, not in Aspen nor in Vegas. A clean break was needed.

He eyed her. "You have plenty of connections. You could use them."

All at once she had an ache in her throat. It sounded like he was beginning to accept her decision. And *that* more than anything showed he really didn't care about her. She was just another employee to him. Nothing more.

"I'm thinking I might get right away from this type of work."

"And do what?"

"I don't know." She took a breath. "In any case, I'd really like to leave Aspen as soon as possible, so that I can wrap up things in Vegas before going home. It shouldn't take more than a couple of days." She'd make sure it didn't.

He scanned her face. "You're not telling me everything," he said, sending her heart bumping against her ribs.

"There's nothing else to tell. I do have a life and a family away from you, Blake, as hard as that may be for you to believe." She couldn't take much more of this. Going over to the desk, she picked up the letter. "So I'd appreciate it if you would accept my resignation." She walked toward him. "Ideally I'd like to leave here as soon as possible. Tomorrow even." Reaching him, she held out the letter.

He didn't take it.

There was a measured silence, then, "No."

The breath stalled in her throat. "Wh-what?"

"No, I won't accept your letter of resignation and certainly not on such short notice. I need you here with me."

His words sent a jet of warmth through her until she remembered this evening. It had been torturous watching him and that actress flirt with each other. How could she stay and keep up the pretence that she didn't want Blake for herself?

She continued to hold the letter out to him. "I can't stay, Blake. I really need to leave."

Now.

Tomorrow.

Certainly no later than that.

He ignored the sheet of paper until she lowered her hand. "I'm the new CEO here, Samantha. It wouldn't be professional of you to leave me in the lurch like this."

She felt bad but it came down to emotional survival. "I know, but there are others quite capable of replacing me. Just contact a high-end employment agency. I'll even do it for you before I go. Someone else would love to work here in Jarrod Ridge. They could be here by Monday."

His mouth tightened. "No."

She lifted her chin. "I'm afraid you have no choice."

"I don't?" he said silkily, inching closer. "You can't quit without a month's notice. It's in your contract."

She sucked in a sharp breath. "Surely you could waive that for me? I've given you two years of my life, Blake, and I've done the job exceptionally well. I've been at your beck and call 24/7. I think you owe me this."

"If you insist on leaving before your contract is up then I'll see you in court." He gave a significant pause. "I don't think that would look good on your résumé, do you?"

"You wouldn't!"

"Wouldn't I?

"This is business," he continued. "Don't take it personally."

She almost choked then. That was the problem. Everything was business between them. *Nothing* was personal.

Her hands shook with anger as she began folding the letter in four. Then she leaned forward and tucked it into his jacket pocket. "Fine. You've got your month. Two weeks here and then two weeks back in Vegas to finish up. After that I'm leaving for Pasadena." She went to step past him.

In a flash he grabbed her arm and stopped her, looking down into her eyes. It was the first time he'd ever touched her *with meaning* and something passed between them. She saw his spark of surprise before he dropped her arm. It surprised her, too.

"I never take no for an answer, Samantha. Remember that."

"There's always the exception to every rule. And I'm it, *Mr. Jarrod*."

* * *

She was still shaking when she got out of the SUV and back to her room at Pine Lodge. She was angry at Blake's refusal to let her go without giving a month's notice, and excited by the awareness in his eyes when he'd touched her. Was she crazy to look more into this than she should?

Her heartbeat stretched into a gallop at the thought that he was attracted to her. A split second was all it had taken and she'd known what it was like to have this man want her. Would he let himself take it further? Remembering the way he'd immediately dropped his hand and withdrawn, she knew he wouldn't.

Yet he'd wanted to, and that was the difference between him and Carl. Oh, she'd had a physical relationship many years ago as a teenager, but looking back, that had been so adolescent. Since then it had only been Carl, and he hadn't wanted her beyond a kiss or two.

But with Blake tonight, she'd known for a moment what it was like for a *man* to really desire her. And that gave her hope that with a bit of encouragement he might make her his. What did she have to lose now? If she went home without taking this opportunity to become Blake's lover she'd always wonder what it would have been like to be kissed by him, to be held by him, to have their bodies joined. And she'd always ache inside for what might have been.

She frowned. How could she capture his attention again and keep it? So far she'd tried everything and nothing had worked. She'd made herself as attractive as possible for him, to no avail. She'd even tried flirting over dinner earlier, but it had fallen faster than a lead balloon. Instead she'd ended up jealous of that actress's ability to flirt so naturally. If only *she* could act like...

Just then a thought clicked in her mind. She couldn't believe she hadn't thought of this before now, but if flirting with Blake hadn't made him sit up and take notice of her, maybe he needed to be stirred up. Maybe he needed an award-winning performance. And a little taste of jealousy.

Yet Blake wasn't the type of man who wanted things made easy for him. Making it appear at least a little difficult to catch her had to be the way to go. He wouldn't be interested otherwise.

And what better way to get his attention than letting him see that other men wanted her? Blake wouldn't be able to resist the challenge. This past week at least two good-looking men had asked her out to dinner but she'd turned them down. She hadn't wanted to be with any man but Blake. She still didn't, but he didn't need to know that.

Starting tomorrow, she'd let herself be wined and dined by men who desired her. She wasn't about to take it any further than that, but she wasn't going to sit around any longer and be uptight Samantha for the rest of her time here either. Sam Thompson was about to break out of her shell.

After Samantha left his office, Blake stood there for a minute, stunned by his encounter with his assistant, and not only because she'd wanted to resign. When he'd touched her he'd had the strongest urge to pull her into his arms and make love to her. She'd felt it, too. He'd seen an acknowledgement in her blue eyes she hadn't been able to hide. Strangely, it excited him. He wasn't used to beautiful women holding themselves back. Women usually *gave* themselves to him.

Clearly it had taken Samantha by surprise as much as it had him. Equally as clearly, she wasn't about to act on it. She probably didn't know *how* to act on it. Over the two years that she'd worked for him he'd rarely seen her date. She was a beautiful woman who socialized with grace and class at functions they both attended, but there had never seemed to be a permanent man in her life. Admittedly *he* kept her busy, but he'd often wondered if she'd had a bad relationship somewhere along the way.

None of that mattered right now, he told himself as he strode over to the window, catching sight of the SUV taking Samantha back the short distance to their private lodge. He waited until the car drove past the cabins and lodges then weaved around a corner and out of sight before letting his thoughts break free.

Damn her.

He didn't often feel thunderstruck, but she'd dropped a bombshell on him tonight. How could she think of leaving him at a time like this? She was his right-hand man. His assistant who made sure everything ran like clockwork. He couldn't do without her and certainly not after coming home to run the resort. He and his younger brother Gavin had already talked about building a new high-security bungalow for their most elite guests in a separate area of the resort.

So why, right when he needed her the most, did Samantha want to bail out on him? He'd expected better of her than desertion. Her excuse that she wanted to go home for a while hadn't made sense. She wasn't one to let her emotions get the best of her anyway and neither was he. That was what he'd liked about her from the start. Now his instincts told him she wasn't telling him the full truth.

Yet if she couldn't be truthful after working closely together, then something was definitely wrong. It just went to remind him to never trust anyone. A person thought they had everything, and in an instant it was gone. Hadn't that been the way since his mother had died from cancer when he was six and his father had withdrawn and blocked everyone out emotionally? It was like both his parents had died at the same time. He'd grown up determined to be totally independent from any emotional entanglements.

Okay, so Donald Jarrod had enough of himself left over to push his five children to be achievers, but at what cost? Four of Donald's offspring had departed years ago to make their mark in other parts of the country. Guy owned a famous French restaurant in Manhattan and ran another business venture. Gavin was a construction engineer. And Melissa was a licensed masseuse who had run a spa and massage-therapy retreat in L.A. Trevor was the only one who'd stayed in Aspen, but had chosen to have nothing to do with the resort, and instead built up his own successful marketing business.

Hell, Blake hadn't seen much of his four younger brothers and sister these past ten years. As his fraternal twin, he was closest to Guy, but he'd still kept a close eye on all his siblings. If they'd needed him, he would have been there. Of course his mind was still out on his half sister, Erica, who'd only recently shown up to become part of the family.

Unfortunately now he needed to rely on *all* of them to make sure the place continued to be a success. It wasn't a feeling he enjoyed. He didn't like relying on anyone, but he'd thought he could count on Samantha.

Obviously he couldn't.

Feeling restless, he looked out over the renowned ski resort that had always been the one place he called home. No matter how much he'd tried to forget it, Jarrod Ridge was in his blood.

He was now the CEO of Jarrod Ridge, for God's sake. His ancestor, Eli Jarrod, had started up the silver mine during the mining boom of 1879, and built himself one of the biggest houses in Colorado. Then "The Panic" of 1893 had closed many of Aspen's mines, and Eli had added to his house and made it bigger, turning it into a grand hotel that was now Jarrod Manor. This place had been through a lot, surviving right through to 1946 when the ski resort idea was born. Jarrod Ridge hadn't looked back since. It was a powerful feeling being in charge of all he surveyed.

And a big responsibility.

And dammit, he wasn't about to let Samantha walk out on him when he needed her most. Even in a month's time he would still need her by his side. It was important to the resort to make sure the changeover went as smoothly as possible, and only Samantha could help him do that. She was the best assistant he'd ever had and he wasn't about to lose her. He would find a way to make her stay, at least until the new bungalow was up and running.

He expelled a breath as he went over to his desk, where he sat down on the leather chair and took the resignation letter out from his jacket pocket. Under the lamplight, he read it, hoping to glean some hint on what was going on inside his assistant's mind. The letter was as professional as expected. No surprises there.

Frowning, he dropped the letter and picked up the pen, rolling it between his fingers as he tried to think. He didn't understand. Surprise appeared to be the name of the game with Samantha right now.

Why?

All at once the metal in his hand went from cool to warm in a matter of seconds, reminding him of his cool and remote assistant who'd soon warmed up at his touch. His heart took a sudden and extra beat. Would Samantha warm up for him if he touched her again? Remembering the electricity between them when he'd grabbed her arm, a surge of need raced through him. Samantha didn't seem to know what she wanted, but he *did* know women. She had wanted him. She had reacted to his touch.

And if that were the case, then perhaps he'd touch her some more and keep her around as long as necessary. He was sure he could persuade her to stay at least another six months. By then they'd both be ready to end the relationship. Sometime in the new year he'd more than likely be over needing her help anyway, and by then he would have someone to replace her, both in the office and the bedroom. No other woman had lasted longer than that. He wouldn't let them. Having affairs was the best he could offer.

As for Samantha, she was independent. She'd have no difficulty moving on when the time came. Hell, she'd probably even instigate it.

For now, it would be his pleasure to awaken the woman in her. Seducing Samantha was definitely going to be a priority task.

TWO

Samantha felt more than a few moments of trepidation when she woke to the early morning light and remembered what she'd done. She'd actually handed Blake her resignation. She would be out of his life in a month's time. She tried to picture being apart from him for the rest of her life, but the thought brought silly tears to her eyes that she quickly blinked back.

Taking a shuddering breath, she tried to put all this in perspective. She'd moved on before, hadn't she? It wasn't so hard. Of course leaving Pasadena had been an adventure as much as an escape. It would be a long time before she escaped wanting Blake Jarrod.

Oh, God.

Then she remembered the plan she'd come up with last night. At the time she'd thought it was brilliant, but now she wasn't so sure she should go out with other men to try and make Blake jealous. It didn't seem right to manipulate the situation like that.

And that left her exactly...nowhere.

Remembering the sizzle of Blake's touch, she wondered if she really wanted to leave without giving them a chance. It was comforting to know that he would not want to get emotionally involved, but to become his lover, to be forever warmed by the memory of being in his arms, didn't she have to do this for herself?

She could do it. This was a goal that was achievable. She may not be a femme fatale but she was considered attractive and she knew how to flirt. And while it may not have worked with Blake at the dinner last night, she knew she could interest other men here in Aspen. Hopefully she'd grab his attention that way.

Tossing back the covers like she was tossing away her shackles, she jumped out of bed. She felt more lighthearted by the minute.

After her shower, Samantha figured it would be prudent to distance herself from Blake as much as possible from now on. She wouldn't capture any man's attention if she was with him all the time.

First things first.

Apart from the maids from the hotel who tidied up Pine Lodge each day, she and Blake had decided to be mostly self-sufficient. The refrigerator was usually stocked with food or they could eat at Jarrod Manor, the main lodge on the resort where some of the family chose to live.

Usually they ate a light breakfast together— surprisingly Blake hadn't brought any women back to the lodge while she'd been here—before they walked the short distance to his father's old office at the Manor. Anything to do with his hotels in Vegas was kept separate and done here in the office they'd set up in a corner of the large living room. That work was mostly done after dinner each evening. There was a lot to do with running both businesses, especially now that it was pre-ski season here. Samantha didn't mind keeping so busy. Besides, it kept Blake close.

But today was different. Fifteen minutes later, she quietly closed the lodge door behind her and left without waiting for him. The Colorado sun was making a shy return as she breathed in crystal air and walked the winding streets in picture-perfect surroundings. As she approached this grandest of hotels, a thrill went through her. With its main stone building complemented by guest wings on both sides, its peaked roofs and balconies with iron railings and its frosted windowpanes, it looked like an enchanted castle.

The doorman greeted her as she entered the hotel from under the stone arch leading off the driveway. She smiled and walked through the wide lobby dotted with tables and chairs. Being the off-season, it was quiet at this time of the morning with only a few guests up and about. A young couple stood viewing photographs of the mountains displayed along the wood walls. Older couples looked ready to go sightseeing the many popular tourist attractions, than pamper themselves in the spa.

It was no better in the casual eatery off the lobby, and Samantha sighed as she scooped scrambled eggs onto a plate from the buffet. Couldn't there have been one measly attractive man in sight this morning? So much for her plans to make Blake jealous. It wouldn't happen if she couldn't even find a man to flirt with.

She lifted her head and saw Blake's half sister, Erica Prentice, come out of the kitchen area and walk through the room with Joel Remy, the resort doctor. Joel was tall, blond and good-looking and he'd asked her out only last week and she'd refused, not giving it any consideration. Things had changed.

Erica saw her and blinked in surprise as she came over to her table. "Samantha, what are you doing here eating breakfast by yourself?"

Samantha liked Erica, who hadn't known she was a member of the Jarrod family until a few months ago. Since then, Erica had become engaged to the Jarrod family attorney, Christian Hanford, and everyone was happy about it. Everyone except Blake, that is, though Guy had taken a while to come round. Erica was a PR specialist who had thrown herself into the running of the resort, willingly giving a hand wherever it was needed, just like the other family members. Samantha didn't understand Blake's attitude toward her.

She smiled at the other woman. "I was up early so I thought I'd get a head start on the boss."

Erica laughed. "Yes, I think as Blake's assistant you'd need to do that occasionally."

Samantha let her eyes slide to the man beside Erica. "Good morning, Joel. You're here early, as well."

The doctor smiled. "One of the kitchen staff burned her hand, but thankfully it was only minor."

Samantha nodded, then, "Where are my manners? Would you like to join me for breakfast? Erica, you, too, of course."

As if she was getting a vibe, Erica glanced from one to the other and went to speak, but Joel got in before her. "I can't, I'm afraid, Sam," the doctor said. "I have to go out on another call. But how about I make it up to you? It's Saturday and my night off. If you're free I'd love to take you to dinner."

Samantha could have kissed him, but she managed to restrain herself. If Blake didn't get jealous over this, then at least she'd have some fun, right?

Thinking of Blake must have made him appear. He was at this moment striding through the lobby with a scowl on his face, heading for the private elevator. Her heart jumped in her throat when he glanced over toward them and saw her in the eatery. He changed direction and advanced toward her.

She turned back to Joel, waiting a few moments more for Blake to get closer. "Dinner tonight?" she said, raising her voice just a little. "Yes, I'd like that very much, Joel."

He grinned at her. "Great. How about I pick you up at seven-thirty?"

"Perfect."

Blake was almost at the table.

"I'd better go see my next patient," Joel said, then inclined his head as he passed by. "Good morning, Blake."

Blake nodded, then stopped at the table and practically glared down at Samantha. "You didn't wait for me."

She reminded herself how this man didn't like things made easy for him. "I slipped a note under your door. Besides, I do believe I start work at nine and until then my time is my own," she said, aware of Erica's speculative gaze.

Blake must have been, too. He darted an irritated look at his half sister, then away, jerking his head at Joel's retreating back. "What did the doctor want?"

Was he jealous already? She felt a thrill of excitement but before she could answer, Erica said, "Joel's taking Samantha out to dinner tonight."

Blake blinked in shock, but he recovered quickly, his blue eyes narrowing in on Samantha. "You can't go. I need you to work for a couple of hours tonight. I'm expecting an important call."

"I'm sorry, Blake, but I'm entitled to some time off."

He shook his head. "Not tonight, I'm afraid. I'd do it myself but as you know, I have a function to attend in town." He regarded her with a hint of smugness in his eyes. "That's why I pay you the big bucks."

Samantha's stomach started to churn. For all that she had wanted him jealous…for all that she anticipated him being difficult with the job…she still hadn't expected he would be quite so obstructive. It was obvious he was going to be exactly that from now on.

Well, she didn't like being told what to do, especially when it was out of spite. Oh, boy, she was going to really enjoy *not* making this easy for him now.

Her chin angled up at him. "Only for the next month," she pointed out smoothly, suddenly wanting to throttle him.

His mouth tightened. "Listen—"

"Blake," Erica's voice cut across him soothingly. "I really think you're being unfair here. If necessary, one of the staff can—"

"Mind your own business, Erica," he snapped, making both Samantha and Erica gasp. He grimaced, a pulse beating in his cheekbone. "Sorry. I shouldn't have said that." Then he looked at Samantha. "Go if you must," he said, then twisted on his heels and stormed off.

"Oh, my God, that was terrible, Erica," Samantha muttered. "I don't know what came over him."

Erica stood watching her half brother storm into the elevator. "I do."

Samantha sighed. "Yes, he seems to have a problem with you, doesn't he? I'm sure he'll be fine once he gets used to having a new sister."

"Half sister," Erica corrected with a wry smile, then sat down on the chair opposite. "Samantha, I don't think it's me who's upset him. What's going on between you two?"

Samantha was unsure how much she should confide in the other woman. When it came down to it, Erica was a Jarrod. Still, the others would have to know sometime. "I've given him my resignation. I finish up in a month's time."

"What! But why?" Erica cried. "I thought you loved your job." She reached across the table and squeezed Samantha's hand. "Please don't leave. I love you being here. You're part of the family."

Samantha felt her heart lift, then take a dive as fast. She'd only just begun to know Blake's family and now she had to leave. "It's time for me to make a change."

Erica gave her a penetrating look. "There's been something bothering you lately." She paused. "Blake needs you, Samantha."

For the job, that was all.

"Yes, he's made it quite clear that's why he's making me work out my contract for the next month." She couldn't stop her lips from twisting. "He told me it's nothing personal."

There was another pause, then, "I see."

Samantha realized she may have said too much. The other woman probably saw more than she should.

All at once Erica gave a disarming smile. "You know what I do when I'm feeling down? I go shopping. How about I take you into town after lunch and we buy you a new dress for tonight?"

Samantha knew Erica was trying to make her feel better. "It's a lovely thought, but I've already got enough dresses. And anyway, I have to work. Blake's going to make sure he gets his money's worth from me from now on."

Erica waved that aside. "I bet most of your clothes are suitable for Vegas, not here. And please…no woman ever has enough dresses," she teased, looking beautiful and happy but still slightly concerned. "Besides, I think it will do Blake good to do without you for a couple of hours." She winked. "He owes me now for being such a jerk."

Samantha appreciated it and she tried to smile but couldn't. "Erica, it's not a good idea." Despite being angry with Blake, she realized she'd probably pushed him a bit too much already today. She'd wanted to shock him into being jealous. Not give him a heart attack!

"Phooey! You want to look good for Joel tonight, don't you?"

Samantha thought about why she'd accepted the invitation to dinner with Joel in the first place. This was about making Blake jealous, she reminded herself, so she still had to keep trying. She couldn't give up after the first try.

She nodded. "Yes, I do."

"Then let's light a fire under him, honey, if that's what he needs."

Samantha did her best not to give anything away, but they both knew Erica was talking about Blake, not Joel. And seeing that this might be her one and only chance…

"Okay then, Erica. I'm in your hands. I have nothing to lose."

"Good girl! I'll come by the office after lunch." Erica got to her feet. "I'd better go and check on the staff member who burned her hand." She smiled and headed back the way she'd come.

As Erica left, Samantha sat for a few moments then looked down at the remains of her scrambled eggs. She just hoped she didn't end up like her breakfast—out in the cold and barely touched.

After lunch Blake's bad mood increased as he watched Erica leave his office, taking his assistant with her for the afternoon. They were going shopping, for Christ's sake! For a dress for Samantha's date tonight!

Damn Erica. His half sister was beautiful and smart, but, unlike his brothers and Melissa, he didn't totally trust her. After listening to her for the last five minutes, he hadn't changed his mind. She was unmistakably adroit at getting her own way, using his outburst this morning against him to make him feel guilty. It had worked like a charm, as she'd known it would.

But it was Samantha he really needed to fathom, he decided, leaning back in the leather chair. He'd woken up thinking he'd go after her with an enthusiasm he rarely felt for a woman these days.

And then it had all gone wrong. First, there had been the note slipped under his door that she'd already gone to breakfast and hadn't waited for him. She'd *never* done that before, not here in Aspen or anywhere else they'd stayed throughout the world.

Then he'd found her accepting a date with that gigolo doctor, Joel Remy. That was like going out with one of the ski instructors. Didn't Samantha know women were lined up to sleep with these guys? He'd seen it all his life.

Take a number, Samantha.

What the hell was going on here? She suddenly seemed a different person. It was like she'd decided to place being a woman first, his assistant second.

What had got into her? Was she trying to pay him back for not letting her walk out on the job early? Would she really *do* that? He grimaced. She was a woman, wasn't she? She'd probably decided to have a farewell fling just to rub his nose in it.

Thoughts of Samantha in bed with another man were suddenly anathema to him. He couldn't let her do it. He *knew* her and he knew she'd regret it.

And surely if she was going to make love to anyone, then she could damn well choose *him*. *He* was the one who'd worked closely with her for two years. *He* was the one who would appreciate her in bed. *He* was the one who had to save her from herself.

Three

As she descended the stairs that evening, carrying her clutch bag in one hand and her cashmere evening coat over her arm, Samantha's foot faltered on the next step. She'd been hoping to show herself off to Blake before he left for his business dinner, and now her heart began knocking against her ribs when she saw the man in question look up from the corner bar in their lodge and catch sight of her. His glass stopped halfway to his mouth and he stared…just stared…as she slowly came the rest of the way down.

Thanks to Erica, she knew she looked fantastic. She'd always taken pride in her appearance and in making sure she looked right for her position, but this long-sleeved dress—this piece of hot-pink knit material that stretched over her body like it had been lovingly cling-wrapped to every curve—made her feel a little naughty.

Without taking his eyes off her, Blake put his drink on

the bar and watched her walk toward him. "I'm stunned," he said in a deep, husky voice that held true admiration and sent her pulse skipping with delight. "I've never seen you look so…"

"Nice?" she gently teased as her confidence soared. She would forgive him anything right at this moment.

"Sexy."

The word took her breath away. She moistened her lips and saw his blue eyes dart to her mouth. "Thank you, Blake."

Then his gaze rolled down her, before slowly coming up again, his eyelids flicking briefly when he passed over her breasts both times. She had the feeling her nipples may have beaded with sexual excitement and one part of her wanted to hunch over and say "don't look," while another forced her to hold her shoulders back proudly.

His eyes—dark with a desire she'd never seen before—finally stopped at her head. "What have you done to your hair?"

She swallowed. It hadn't taken much to style the silky brown strands into bouncing curls around her shoulders. "I had a couple of inches cut off it."

"It looks terrific."

This was the reaction she'd been hoping for from him. "Thank you again."

He picked up his drink and took a sip. Then, "I have to ask you something."

Her heart took a leap. "What is it, Blake?"

"Are you sure you want to do this?"

She blinked. "Do what?"

Resign?

"Go out with Joel Remy."

His voice gave nothing away but her pulse started

to race even more. Dear God, could Blake be a little jealous? Had she actually managed to get through to him so quickly that she was a woman? A woman who needed him like she'd never needed any man before?

His eyes slammed into her. "He's not your style, Samantha."

Her heart almost burst through her chest. Blake *was* jealous. She tried to act nonchalant. She couldn't succumb and throw herself at him the minute he decided he wanted her for five minutes.

"How do you know *what* my style is, Blake?" she said, fluttering her eyelashes at him.

"I know what suits you and what doesn't and I know he's not the man for you."

No, this man in front of her was the man for her.

"Oh, so you're an expert on me now, are you?" she flirted, thrilled beyond her wildest dreams that he was finally noticing her. It was this dress. She had so much to thank Erica for. The other woman had…

"I'd like to think I know you very well, Samantha," he said, suddenly looking very superior, very arrogant. "You wouldn't be happy with Remy. Trust me."

Thud.

Clarity hit her like a bolt of lightning. What a fool she was in thinking anything had changed. This wasn't about Blake wanting her. This was about him being his usual conceited self. The man wasn't jealous. He was merely trying to stop her having a relationship with another man over the next two weeks so that she wouldn't inconvenience *him*. Frankly, she deserved better than this.

"That's your considered opinion, is it?" she said coolly now.

"Yes, it is." His eyes told her he'd noticed her change in tone. "Are you going to tell him you're leaving soon?"

She tried to think. She was *so* disappointed. "I'd prefer to keep that to myself for the time being. It's no one's business but my own."

"And mine, of course," he pointed out dryly. Then, "But you're probably right in not telling him. I doubt he's after a long-term relationship anyway."

"Neither am I," she said, taking pleasure in the way his face hardened. "In the meantime, I'm sure Joel and I will both manage to enjoy ourselves."

He looked all-knowing. "I doubt you'll have anything in common."

She raised one eyebrow. "Really? Don't forget I worked in a doctor's office before coming to work for you. And my family runs a medical transcription business, so I used to have quite a bit to do with doctors."

Blake's lips twisted. "So you'll talk about deciphering his handwriting? That'll be a laugh a minute."

Her fingers tightened on her clutch purse. He thought he was being clever, did he? She needed to wipe away that smirk. She gave him a sultry look. "Oh, I'm sure we'll have plenty of…*other things* in common."

The smirk fell off his face. "Dammit, Samantha, you shouldn't—"

The doorbell buzzed.

Samantha glanced over at the front door a few feet away and saw Joel through the glass panel. She tossed Blake an expressive look before going over to open it.

Joel stepped inside, his eyes sliding down, then up. "Wow! Don't you look like a million dollars." He grinned at Blake a few feet away. "I can't believe this beauty is going out with me."

"Neither can I," Blake muttered, then as quickly gave a smooth smile but Samantha heard him. "I mean, she's usually picky about who she goes out with."

She blinked. Was that still an insult? Joel had a puzzled look that said he might be thinking the same thing.

She hurriedly forced a smile. "Thanks for the compliment, Joel." She stood and looked him up and down, too. "For the record, you look like a *billion* dollars," she joked, then realized she'd overplayed her hand when Blake sniffed, though she suspected it was more of a snort. She turned her head slightly so Joel couldn't see her stabbing her boss with her eyes.

Blake ignored her. "So, where are you two dining tonight?"

Samantha was immediately suspicious. "Why do you want to know?"

He smiled. "No reason."

Joel then mentioned a restaurant in the center of Aspen. "It's only just opened and I know the owner. It'll be very hard to get a reservation in another month or so." He didn't sound like he was bragging, at least not to Samantha, but she saw a glint in Blake's eyes that told her he wasn't in agreement.

She smiled at Joel. "That sounds lovely."

He looked pleased. "And you, Blake? You're off to dinner, too, by the look of things."

Wearing a dark suit, Blake was the one who really did look like a billion dollars, Samantha had to admit, unable to stop herself from wishing she was going out with him instead of Joel, in spite of the fact that Blake was being an overbearing jerk.

"Just a business dinner in town." Blake looked at his

watch. "As a matter of fact, I'd better call a cab. I need to be on my way."

Joel frowned. "A cab? Don't you have a car?"

"I noticed it was leaking oil this afternoon so I thought I'd better not use it tonight."

Samantha sensed Blake was manipulating the situation for his own benefit again. Did he think she was stupid? He was doing this on purpose to try and keep her and Joel apart as much as possible to spoil her night.

She stared at him. "But you only bought the vehicle a few months ago and it's barely been used. How can a luxury Cadillac SUV have an oil leak already?"

He looked totally guileless. "I agree. It's the darnedest thing."

"We could give you a lift, if you like," Joel said, making Samantha want to rattle him.

"Oh, I'm sure Blake doesn't want to ride with us." She was determined not to give her boss any satisfaction. "The resort has a chauffeur service."

Joel frowned. "No, that's okay. I don't mind. We're going that way anyway."

She would have sounded mean-spirited to refuse. As Blake well knew, she decided, watching the satisfaction in his eyes. He was Joel's boss and he knew Joel wouldn't deny doing a favor for him.

She passed her coat to Joel. "Would you mind helping me on with this, please?"

"Of course." Joel held it open while she slipped into it, then he helped lift her hair out from under the collar so that it was once again bouncing around her shoulders. It was somewhat intimate and Samantha felt a little awkward at having a man touch her hair, but she soon felt better when she saw the steely look in Blake's eyes after he noted it, too.

"Thanks," she said, smiling brightly at her date, then deliberately linked her arm with his. She gave Blake a sweet smile as he put on his black evening coat, letting him know she didn't care that he wasn't pleased. Too bad!

"My car's out front," Joel said.

They left the lodge, then Samantha slipped onto the front passenger seat before Blake could take it himself. She wouldn't put it past him to try and make her sit in the back, and she wasn't about to let him play at being boss while she was on a date. This was *her* night out. Blake may have been the reason for it, but right now she wasn't about to give him an inch.

Soon they were driving off into the night.

"This is very good of you, Joel," Blake said, sounding grateful from the backseat, which didn't sound right to Samantha's ears. Blake *never* sounded grateful like other mere mortals.

"We don't mind, do we, Sam?" Joel said, shooting her a sideways smile.

"No, of course not. We have to keep the boss happy, don't we?" She smiled back at Joel, knowing Blake could see her from his diagonal viewpoint behind the driver's seat.

"By the way, *Samantha*," Blake said, placing the slightest emphasis on her name, making her realize that Joel had called her "Sam" again—the name Blake had never called her.

"Yes, Blake?" she said, keeping her tone idle.

There was a tiny pause before he spoke. "Don't worry about that very important phone call I was waiting for tonight. One of the resort staff will sit in the office and wait for it."

"Good." She took her job seriously, but Erica's suggestion had been a good one, so she wasn't about to feel guilty about it.

"But I did have to give them your cell phone number, as well. Just in case. I hope you don't mind. Someone has to take the call if by chance it's missed at the hotel, and I'll have to turn my cell phone off so it won't interrupt the guest speaker tonight."

She could feel herself stiffen. He was trying to take advantage of her good nature for his own purposes again. This wasn't about taking the call. He wanted to put a spoke between her and Joel's budding relationship, freeing up her time for the job.

She turned her head to face him. "Actually I *do* mind. This is my night off. I don't want to work tonight."

He raised an eyebrow, like he was surprised. "I'm sure Joel won't have a problem with it. He's a doctor. He's used to being on call. You understand, don't you, Joel?"

"Sure I do." Joel glanced at her and smiled. "Leave your cell phone on, Sam. I don't mind if you take the call."

Her mouth tightened but she didn't reply. Her cell phone was already off and she intended it to stay that way. And Blake knew this had nothing to do with Joel anyway. Blake was just trying to make sure the job was in her face tonight.

Joel must have sensed something amiss because he started talking about general things for the rest of the way. Samantha could feel Blake's eyes on her from the backseat but she ignored him as she responded to Joel, relieved when the car slid to a halt outside a restaurant.

"Thanks for the ride." Blake opened the back door then paused briefly. "And don't worry about how I'll get home. You two have a good time, okay?"

Samantha bit down on her irritation. His sincerity was so false. He was just trying to get a ride back to the lodge to make sure nothing sexual happened between her and Joel. Ooh, it would do him good to wonder and worry what she and Joel were getting up to later in the evening.

She smiled tightly. "We'll be very late, so you'd best get the car service. Good night, Blake."

His lips flattened and he shot her a dark look. "Good night." He waited a second, but when Joel said good night, he got out of the car and shut the door. The last Samantha saw was him striding into the restaurant.

Then they drove off and she looked ahead, hoping Joel wouldn't say anything. He didn't, at least not until they were seated at their table and the waitress had left with their order.

"Excuse me for asking, but don't you like Blake?" he said.

She smiled to soften her words. "Of course I do, but I've worked with Blake a couple of years now. Sometimes he thinks everyone is there purely for his benefit."

Joel grinned. "As a successful businessman, he's probably right."

She laughed. "Yes, that's true." Then she forced herself to relax against the back of her chair. "Now let's talk about something else. I really don't want to talk about the boss tonight."

Joel smiled. "I'm more than happy to oblige, Sam. Now tell me…"

They had a pleasant evening after that. As predicted, they talked about her family's business and her experience in transcribing, though Blake's earlier derogatory comment about deciphering handwriting spoiled the discussion for her. Did Blake always have to be there at the back of her mind?

Unfortunately by the time the evening was half over, Samantha knew Joel wasn't for her. He was handsome and he was a nice guy, but they really *didn't* have anything else in common, much to her disgust. Not like her and Blake. She grimaced. No, she and Blake had nothing in common either—except the job and an attraction that she hated to think was really only on her side. Shades of Carl came to mind.

"Sam?"

She pulled herself back from thoughts of the past. "Sorry, I remembered something I forgot to do," she fibbed, then she smiled. "But it can wait. Now, what were you saying?" She would have a good time if it killed her.

It nearly did.

Her social life and her work life were the same thing, so she'd never lacked for company at business dinners and parties. But she wasn't used to being on a date and having to tune in to one person for hours on end. It was very draining.

Unless of course that person was Blake. He never bored her. Every minute of every day he challenged her like no other person on earth. Life with Blake was the adventure she'd always been after. One she soon had to leave, she remembered, her heart constricting. She pushed the thought aside. She would get through this.

"We should do this again, Sam," Joel said, holding open his car door for her on their return to Pine Lodge.

It was strange, but for some reason an evening of being called "Sam" had started to get on her nerves. It wasn't Joel's fault at all, but it was as if the shortened version of her name was an issue between her and Blake and therefore belonged only to them now. And that was rather pathetic.

"I've got plans tomorrow night," Joel said, dragging her from her thoughts. "But I'm free after that. Would you like to go to a movie on Monday night?"

She hesitated, feeling a little bad in using him. She didn't want to go out with him again, yet if she didn't continue with her plan to try and make Blake jealous, then Blake would think he'd won. She wouldn't give him the satisfaction now.

She got out of the car, with Joel doing the gentlemanly thing and assisting her. "I'd like that, but let me get back to you tomorrow, if that's okay."

"That's fine."

All at once she felt his hand move from her elbow to her chin. It was a smooth move and said this guy knew what he was doing, so perhaps using him shouldn't really cause her concern after all.

"But first…" he murmured.

She didn't resist even though his kiss wasn't something she wanted, and not because he wasn't an attractive man. Despite still being angry with Blake for trying to manipulate the situation earlier this evening, she wanted it to be Blake's lips—and *only* Blake's lips—on hers.

Suddenly scared that she might never want another man to kiss her, she raised her mouth to Joel. Perhaps Blake's attraction for her was merely in her mind? Perhaps she needed to be kissed by another man just to remind her—

"Don't let me interrupt," a male voice muttered.

Blake.

Samantha jerked back guiltily and Joel stopped, and they watched their employer stride past them and go inside Pine Lodge. He'd been walking from the direction of Jarrod Manor, where he must have gone after dinner.

"That was good timing," Joel said, over her thudding heart. Unfortunately her heart's thud wasn't for her date. It was for another man.

"Now, where were we?" Joel murmured, lowering his head and placing his lips on hers, making her conscious of one thing. She'd have to stretch her neck higher if it was Blake kissing her.

Blake sat on the couch and tried to get the image of Samantha about to kiss another man out of his head. She'd been swaying toward the doctor like she'd needed a shot in the arm. If she didn't get inside here pretty damn quick he was going looking for her. On the pretext of her safety, of course.

And he *was* concerned for her safety. That and other things. She was clearly ready to jump into bed with the first man who looked twice at her, and all to get back at *him* for not letting her walk away from her job. Hell, if he'd agreed to that she would have already gone from his life. His gut twisted at the thought.

The front door opened right then and in she walked. His pulse began to race when he saw she was alone.

Good girl.

She seemed distracted as she headed for the stairs, undoing the buttons of her coat as she walked. Then she saw him sitting on the couch and her eyes flared with pleasure before she seemed to catch herself.

For a moment his breath stalled. She'd never shown any sort of emotion toward him before. They got on well together but it had always been business between them. He should be perturbed, yet he knew he could use it to his advantage.

Then her mouth tightened as she came toward him. "Are you waiting up for me?" she said, her tone less than friendly, making him question if it had been a trick of the light before. He mentally shook his head. No, he knew what he'd seen.

"Can't a man have a drink before bed?" he drawled, relaxing. She was home now…with him…and that's all that mattered.

Her top lip curled. "You certainly didn't have to worry about drinking and driving, did you?"

He pretended ignorance. "No, I didn't." He indicated another glass of brandy on the coffee table in front of him. "I poured a nightcap for you. Sit with me."

An odd look skimmed across her face. "Perhaps I'd prefer to go straight to bed."

If one of his dates had said that he would have taken it as a come-on. But Samantha was a challenge in a different way. Did she know what she was inviting in that dress? Did she have any idea what she actually did to a man's libido? All at once he was enjoying what he now suspected to be her sexual naïveté.

"One drink," he coaxed. "And you can tell me all about your evening."

She paused, then put down her evening purse and began undoing the rest of her coat buttons. Slowly she began taking it off in an unintentional striptease, exposing the sexy pink material beneath. How had he never before noticed what a stunner she was?

She sank down on the opposite chair and gracefully picked up the glass, indicating the already poured brandy. "You were so sure I wouldn't take Joel up to my room, were you?"

He hadn't been, no. "Yes."

She took a sip then considered him. "You certainly tried hard enough to make it *not* happen."

"Did I?" He was feeling rather proud of himself for putting obstacles in her way tonight. It must have worked or she wouldn't be here now. With him.

"You know you did, and I don't appreciate it. You're trying to make sure you get every last bit of work out of me before I leave."

Is that what she thought? "Maybe I was protecting you?"

She gave a short laugh. "From what? Having a good time?"

He looked over at her kissable lips that had recently been beneath another man's…and something became even more determined inside him. If she was going to have fun, she was going to have it with *him*.

He forced a shrug. "I just think you need to look at who you go out with in future."

Her lips twisted. "Thanks for the tip."

He'd never known her to be sarcastic, not like she was lately. It was…energizing, he admitted, watching as she eased back in her chair, the soft silk stockings making a swishing sound as she crossed her legs. He'd give anything to reach out and smooth those long legs with his hands. Or perhaps his lips…

Before he could put words to action, he told himself he had to slow it down. He didn't want to frighten the lady by going too quickly. Time was running out but he had to let her lead. Tonight, anyway. Tomorrow—when she was in a friendlier mood—was another day.

He took a sip of his brandy and let it soothe his throat. "So. Did you have a good time tonight?"

Her eyes darted away briefly. "Yes, I did. Very much."

She was lying. "I bet."

She arched one of her elegant eyebrows. "I hope you didn't put much money on that bet, Blake."

"I didn't have to." He knew women, both in the business world and out of it. She was lying. And he was intensely relieved.

A soft smile curved her lips. "Joel really knows how to treat a woman."

She was still lying. And he found that fascinating. "Sure he knows how to treat a woman. The guy's a womanizer."

"I suppose it's easy enough to recognize one's own sort."

He had to chuckle. She made him laugh. Then he saw a touch of real amusement in her eyes and something connected between them. She quickly looked down at her glass, hiding her eyes for a second.

He started to lean forward. "Samantha…"

Her head snapped up. "For your information, Joel's a

very nice man," she said, making it clear she was trying to ignore the sudden sexual tension in the room.

It was a wasted effort. "I'm sure he is. Ask *any* woman in Aspen."

She sent him a defiant look. "Don't think I wouldn't go to bed with him if I wanted to, Blake."

She was all talk, but his gut still knotted at her words. "Obviously you didn't want to, or you would be in bed with him this very minute. Am I right?"

"No, you're wrong. I mean, yes… I mean, mind your own business." Her lips pressed together. "I'll sleep with whoever I want *when* I want."

"You're being very contradictory tonight, Samantha. They'd eat you alive in the boardroom with that attitude," he mocked.

She stiffened. "Listen, Blake, I'll sleep with any man I want when I'm good and ready. Tonight I just wasn't ready. And in case you didn't notice, this isn't the boardroom."

No, but he did want to eat her alive right now. He wanted to kiss her and take away the imprint of another man's lips, his hands itching to slide up over her hot dress and lift that hair off her nape himself, exposing the soft skin beneath to his lips.

Adrenaline pumping through him, he knew it was time to take action. He'd had enough playing games tonight. He wasn't one to sit on the sidelines for long. He needed to know if her lips were as good as they looked, if her body would curve to his touch, if the skin at her nape was soft and sensitive.

Surging to his feet, he removed the brandy glass from her hand and put it on the table. He heard her intake of breath as he pulled her to her feet, but nothing would stop him now. Already he could feel a mutual shudder pass between them.

"Blake?" she said huskily as he brought her into the circle of his arms, leaving mere inches between them. He'd never been this close to her before. Not close enough to see the rush of desire in her blue eyes. It knocked the breath from his body.

And then a sudden flash of panic swept her face and before he knew it, she had pushed against him and spun away. Scurrying toward the stairs, she left him standing there, his arms never feeling as empty as they did right now.

As hard as it was, he let her go. He could follow her and she would take him as her lover, but he knew all he needed to know for the moment. She wanted him. And he wasn't giving up. His plans for seduction were still very much alive.

Samantha closed the door behind her and pressed herself back against it, willing her racing heart to slow down so that she could let herself think. She'd gone and panicked just now. Blake had finally reached for her and she'd blown it.

What was wrong with her! Being in Blake's arms and in his bed was what she wanted most, wasn't it? So why had she run away like a frightened deer? He must think her green when it came to relationships, which of course she was. One lover in high school, then falling in love in her mid-twenties, did not constitute experience. Not unless that included the pain of rejection, she decided, quickly pushing that thought away.

Then she knew.

Despite the spark of electricity when he'd grabbed her

arm last night, this evening she'd managed to convince herself that his meddling was actually about the job and nothing more. But just now the desire in his eyes had thrown her for a loop again. He really *did* feel passion for her, and when he'd touched her they'd both felt that zip of attraction. It had overwhelmed her, that's all.

Oh, Lord, what did she do now? Go back downstairs and beg him to make love to her? She couldn't. She'd reached the limit to her little seductress act tonight. She didn't have it in her to face him again so soon.

She took a steadying breath. Right, she'd messed this one up tonight, but something positive had come out of this. She now knew that Blake really *did* want to have sex with her. So if she wanted Blake, and he wanted her, then next time there should be no further problems.

She hoped.

Four

"Blake, did you get a chance to read those documents I gave you?"

Blake was in a good mood as he leaned back against the marble countertop. It was eight on Sunday morning and one of his younger brothers had come by Pine Lodge to discuss an upcoming project, but it was Samantha who was on his mind. Anticipation coursed through him as he remembered how sexy she had looked last night. Soon she would be *his*.

"Blake?"

Reluctantly he dragged his thoughts away from his assistant who was still upstairs sleeping in her room, to look at the man propped against the kitchen doorjamb. He hid a smile as he raised the coffee mug to his mouth. Gavin may look laidback but *he* knew it was all a facade. Taking on the job of building a new and exclusive high-security bungalow for Jarrod Ridge meant a lot to his brother.

"Yes. I've put them in the safe up at the Manor," he said, deliberately misunderstanding him.

"And?"

Blake chuckled and put him out of his misery. "And I think you've done an admirable job of running with this project."

Gavin began to smile with relief. "You do?"

"The intensive feasibility studies, as well as the building site and sustainability analysis reports you've put together, are impressive. But then, so were the ones you did for my Vegas hotels."

Gavin's grin widened. "It means a lot to hear you say that."

Blake indicated the coffeepot on the bench. "Grab yourself a coffee."

Gavin straightened away from the door and went to get a mug. "You know," he said, pouring himself a drink. "I've really welcomed this challenge."

"I can see that."

Gavin shrugged shoulders made impressive by many hours working with his crew on various construction sites. "It's nice to be home and together again as a family after so long, but I'm glad I don't have to pamper people on a daily basis. It really isn't my style."

Blake nodded. "You're a first-rate construction engineer, Gav, but I agree. There's nothing like doing something you love."

Gavin smiled, looking pleased. "You said it, brother."

"Seriously. I'm proud of you."

"You getting soft in your old age, Blake?" he teased.

"Probably." Blake was proud of all his brothers and sisters. Well, his half sister, Erica, was another matter.

All at once, Gavin's smile left him. "You realize Dad would never have said such a thing."

Blake grimaced. "I like to think I'm not quite as cold as the old man."

There was a moment's silence as they both remembered their father. Blake refused to feel anything for the passing of a man who had shunned his children's emotional well-being and so badly let them down. Donald Jarrod's legacy had been more than the Jarrod Ridge Resort. It had been a legacy that his children keep their emotions on ice, avoiding personal commitment. And while both Guy and Melissa had found true happiness with Avery and Shane, Blake couldn't see it happening for himself. Not at all. Nor for Gavin or Trevor either. That was just the way it was.

"That reminds me," Gavin said. "You're working out of Dad's old office now you're CEO, so wouldn't it be more convenient to be living at the Manor, as well? Why are you staying here at Pine Lodge instead?"

Blake shrugged. "Actually it's more convenient to be staying here. That way I can keep my hotel operations separate from the resort stuff." His hand tightened around the coffee mug. "Besides, even though Erica's moved into Christian's place, they both spend most of their time at the Manor during the day. I don't want to encroach on their territory. You know what newly engaged couples are like."

Gavin shot him a mocking smile. "Since when have

you ever taken a backseat to anyone, big brother? Or are you still scared of our new half sister?"

Blake knew Gavin was riling him, getting him back for stringing it out a few minutes ago. "I was never scared of Erica, as you well know."

"You're going to have to get over your dislike of her one day, buddy."

Blake felt an odd jolt. "I don't dislike her. I just don't totally trust her."

Gavin's eyes narrowed. "She really doesn't have to prove anything more to us, Blake." He paused. "But I guess it's all for the best that you stay here anyway. Your new assistant might not get on with the rest of the family as well as Samantha does." A speculative look entered his eyes. "Yeah, whoever is coming in as your new PA, it'll be much easier for them to keep the two businesses separate if you both stay here."

Blake's jaw clenched. He refused to even think about Samantha leaving, or someone coming in to replace her. And why was he surprised that word had gotten around the family? Samantha had said she didn't want anyone to know, but obviously she'd told one person at least. It had to have been Erica. No doubt the two had shared some girl talk yesterday while they'd been shopping together.

"Samantha is *not* leaving," he said tightly.

"That's not what I'm hearing."

"Shut up, Gav." He slammed down his half-empty coffee mug. "Now, if you'll excuse me, I have some work to do." He strode past his brother and out of the kitchen.

As he entered the living room, he heard a noise outside. He glanced through the picture window.

Samantha wasn't in bed asleep like he'd thought. She was standing on the bottom step of the lodge, dressed in warm clothes and a woolen hat, talking to a man who no doubt was one of the guests at the hotel. She must have gone up to the Manor to eat breakfast, probably with her doctor friend, and this guy must have followed her back like a lost puppy. No, make that a raccoon.

He heard her give a lilting laugh and his mouth flattened. The guy was in his forties and looked sleazy to Blake. And hell, Samantha looked like she was flirting with him. Didn't she have any sense when it came to men? The sooner he showed her what it was like to make love to *him,* the better.

"Look at that," Gavin murmured in his ear. "I think someone else may be working today...*on* Samantha."

Blake glared at him, then strode over and pulled open the front door in a rush. If she was going to flirt it would be with *him.*

"How about us going for a scenic drive?" the man was saying. "Maybe even do lunch in town? I know it's pretty quiet at this time of year, but we should be able to find somewhere to eat. What do you think?"

"I—"

"I think I need to speak to my assistant," Blake cut across her as he stepped out on the porch. They spun to look up at him. "Samantha, I need you to make some calls to Vegas for me."

She sent him an annoyed look, making it clear she didn't like the interruption. "Blake, it's Sunday and most of the offices are closed. It'll have to wait until tomorrow."

He had the urge to remind her that last night he could easily have taken her to his bed. She wouldn't have minded *that* interruption, he was sure. "Then I need you to help me with something else."

Her lips tightened. "So I'm not going to get any time off now until I leave?"

"No." He turned to go inside and waited but realized she wasn't behind him. "Coming, Samantha?"

Her chin tilted stubbornly. "I'll be there in a minute."

Blake saw Gavin's look of amusement as his brother pushed through the doorway then descended the stairs two at a time, calling out a greeting to the pair as he left.

Blake went back inside. He didn't hear her following. Counting to ten, he waited but he could see her still standing there chatting. At that moment something occurred to him. Wasn't it strange that she'd been jumpy with *him* last night, yet she seemed perfectly at ease with Mr. Sleazy down there? And what about last night with the doc? She hadn't seemed nervous around the guy.

So what did that tell him? That she was flirting with men she considered *safe?* Which meant she must feel nothing for them, he mused. Nothing at all. The thought filled him with relief.

As for what she was feeling for him…there was definitely something between them. Yeah, she knew they'd be explosive together in bed.

And that begged the question. Just how far was she prepared to go to fight her desire for him? More importantly right now, did she have any idea what she was inviting by leading those other two men on?

Making a decision, Blake pulled on his jacket and boots, grabbed his car keys and strode back out into the chilly air. "I need to go check on something," he said, going down the stairs, "and I want you to come with me, Samantha." He bared his teeth at the other man in the semblance of a smile. "Sorry, buddy, but I need my assistant."

"Blake—" she began.

"This is important." He cupped her elbow and began leading her toward the side of the lodge to the garage where he kept his black Cadillac SUV.

She glanced over her shoulder and called out to the other man. "I'll talk to you when I get back, Ralph."

Blake gave a snort as he clicked the remote to open the garage door.

"What was that for?" Samantha hissed, hurrying to keep up.

"I hope you're not thinking of dating *Ralph*. The guy's old enough to be your father. Hell, he's even got a name to match."

She hid her satisfaction. "Perhaps I'm attracted to older men?"

He sent her a knowing look. "Then you'd better not dress like you did last night. He doesn't look like his old ticker could handle a woman, let alone a sexy one like yourself."

Her own "ticker" jumped around inside her chest and she tried not to blush. She loved hearing that Blake thought her sexy, though she wasn't sure why he was looking so confident all of a sudden. Still, this time she wasn't going to run away from him if he made a move on her. No repeat of last night, she told herself firmly.

They entered the garage, but it was only after she slid onto the passenger seat of the SUV and was putting on her seat belt did she remember something. "Didn't you say this vehicle had an oil leak?"

Blake smirked at her. "Here's the thing. I took another look earlier and it wasn't leaking after all. The problem must have been with someone else's car."

"Now there's a surprise."

"It was to me, too," he drawled, starting the engine.

No wonder he looked pleased with himself, she decided. He'd orchestrated the "poor me" routine last night over the oil leak, and now he'd put a stop to her going out with Ralph. Not that Ralph was her type, though he seemed very nice, but he *was* a man and one she could flirt with for Blake's benefit.

Once the vehicle had warmed up, she took off her gloves as he reversed out of the garage.

"Where are we going?" she asked, when he started along the narrow road lined with thick trees, and it became clear they were heading for the main entrance to the resort.

"You'll see."

For a second she dared hope this might be about spending some time alone together away from everyone else. "Is this really about work?"

"What else?"

Disappointment wound its way through her. They were clearly still employer and employee. Had last night merely been an aberration on his part because of the late night and close proximity? Was this once again about Blake trying to stop her from leaving her job, rather than him actually wanting her?

Back to square one.

Soon Blake was driving past the two stone pillars with the brass Jarrod Ridge Resort sign, and turning the SUV onto the main road but in the other direction of town. At this time on a Sunday morning there wasn't much traffic and further along he took another turn onto a side road. She wondered where they were going as they drove through stunning natural scenery filled with golden fall colors that would soon disappear under winter-white, but it was no use asking him again. Blake only did what he wanted to do and he would tell her only what he wanted her to know.

Remembering Gavin had visited Pine Lodge this morning, she suspected then where they were going. Farther along, Blake pulled over onto a slot of land that looked out over the Roaring Fork River weaving its way through a lush green picturesque valley between towering snow-dabbled peaks. The Jarrod Ridge resort was nestled like a crown jewel amongst it all.

He stopped the vehicle and cut the engine.

He didn't speak at first, just stared straight ahead, so she had to ask the obvious. "Why did you bring me here?"

He nodded his dark head at the majestic mountain panorama before them. "I wanted to show you where the new private bungalow will be built."

"I see." Her suspicions were correct, but the way he spoke made her heart sink. It was as if he had acknowledged she was leaving now. Like he was showing it to her—while he still could.

"Let's take a closer look." He started to get out of the car then glanced back at her, his gaze going to the woolen hat on her head. "Put your gloves on first. There's no wind but it's chilly."

A couple of seconds later they were standing in front of the black SUV, looking at the breathtaking alpine backdrop in front of them.

He pointed to a wooded area near the bottom of the

mountain to the right of the resort. "See that over there? That's our silver mine where we used to play as kids. One of my ancestors started up the mine but it's been out of use for over a hundred years."

"How interesting," she said, meaning it.

"The bungalow will be farther up the mountain but not too close. We don't want to destroy the historical significance of the mine."

She'd briefly seen the documents Gavin had given Blake, and heard them discussing it at times, but Gavin was the one running with this project. He was keeping it very much between himself and Blake at this stage, though she knew they were keeping the rest of the Jarrods up to date.

"See that rocky outcropping?" Blake continued. "That's close to where we'll build the bungalow. It's going to be super luxurious with top-of-the-line security. There'll be iris-recognition scanners plus the usual cameras and motion detectors. Personal safety will be a must, as will our guests' privacy."

She could picture it in her mind. "I'm really impressed. It'll be great."

He nodded. "It's just what Jarrod Ridge needs to stand out above the rest," he said, a proud look about him as he appraised his family's empire.

An odd tenderness filled her as she glanced up at his familiar profile. There was something so attractive about a man confident with himself. An aura that pulled a woman close and made her want to get under it, to become a part of the man no one else knew.

All at once he turned toward her, his gaze fixing in on her. "Why are you looking at me like that?" he asked quietly.

Caught!

She cleared her throat. "I was thinking how much you enjoy a challenge. You're suited to these mountains."

He looked pleased. Then, "You could be a part of all this, too, you know."

Her heart stumbled. Had he brought her here for another reason? "Wh-what do you mean?"

"You love it here. You won't be happy anywhere else." He paused. "Think carefully before you walk away from your job, Samantha."

The job.

She groaned inwardly at her stupidity. Had she really thought this confirmed bachelor had been about to pop the marriage question to his personal assistant? What on earth was the matter with her? Hadn't she learned her lesson with Carl? The thin air must be making her imagine things that weren't and could never be. Not that she'd ever consider it anyway.

She took a shuddering breath before speaking. "I *have* thought about it, Blake." Very much so. She hadn't stopped.

He turned to face her. "Stay, Samantha."

"I…I can't." If it had been a plea, she might have considered it. As it was, she knew this was basically still about him being inconvenienced.

She went to turn away. She couldn't face him fully. The last thing she wanted was him seeing she'd mistakenly assumed he was talking marriage a minute ago. What a fool she was for even thinking it, let alone believing he might be thinking it, too. This wasn't about anything more than desire, she reminded herself.

His fingers slid around her arm and tugged her back. "Why are you being so obstructive?"

She couldn't feel the pressure of his fingers through her thick jacket but she knew they were there. "Obstructive to what?"

"To me being concerned for your well-being."

She ignored the thud of her heart. "Oh, so *that's* why you won't let me finish up my job early?" she scoffed, knowing this was the only way she could handle him. "You're *concerned* for me?"

He froze.

Silence surrounded them.

Then, he said quietly, "I am, actually."

She gasped midbreath. "Why, Blake? Why are you concerned for me?"

"Why wouldn't I be?" As he spoke she could feel his eyes almost pulling her toward him.

"Um…Blake…"

He drew her toward him and bent his head. He was kissing her before she knew what was happening, instantly destroying any defenses she may have drawn on, regardless that she wanted him so very much. Like an avalanche rolling down a mountain, she fell—and it was just as devastating.

Then he slid his tongue between her lips and she opened her mouth to him fully. Hearing his husky groan, she wound her arms around his neck and held on to him, trusting him, knowing where he took her she would follow.

Time blurred.

And then, amazingly, he was slowing things down, giving her back herself, letting her regain focus. Finally, he eased back and they stared at each other.

"Oh, my God!" she whispered, awed by the sheer

complexity of the kiss that should have been simple and wasn't. It left her trembling.

He was feeling something equally as powerful. She could see it deep in his eyes. He truly desired her. Her dream of being in his arms was finally becoming a reality.

His cell phone began to ring.

He remained still, not moving, and she knew why. Nothing could take away from the strength of this moment between them. Here in the mountains it was like they were the only two people alive.

Then as quickly as she thought that, he blinked and turned away, breaking the moment. She heard him answer it, but she couldn't seem to move. She understood why he had turned away. Why he had broken the moment. It had been too much for him. For her. For them both. Without him looking at her, she could take a breath again.

She did.

And then she found she could move. She swiveled to go get into the SUV, needing to sit down for a minute and feel something solid beneath her.

She took a few steps but as she went to reach for the door handle, her feet slipped from under her on a patch of ice and, with a small cry, she felt herself falling backward…backward….

She frantically made a grab for anything within reach, but there was only the air and she felt her legs going up and her body going down, her back hitting the grass, then her head on something harder. She literally saw stars….

The next thing she knew Blake was dropping to his knees beside her. "Thank God!" he muttered, when he saw her eyes were open.

"What happened?" she managed to say.

He glanced back to where she'd been walking. "You must have slipped on that ice back there."

She started to lift her head, then winced at the pain.

"Take it slowly." He put his hand under her shoulders to help her up. "Is your back sore or anything? Are you hurting anywhere?"

"No."

Then he swore. "You're bleeding."

"I am?"

His hand came away with some blood on it. "You've cut your head." He helped her to sit up, then he checked the back of her head. "It's only small but it's bleeding like the devil and might need a stitch. There's a lump starting where you hit it, too." Snatching up her woolen hat that must have come off during the fall, he placed it against the cut. "Hold that on it. It'll help stem the flow of blood. We need to get you to a doctor."

"Joel?" she said, without thinking, not meaning anything by it.

His mouth tightened. "Yes." He waited. "Do you think you can stand up? Are you dizzy or anything?"

"A little, but I'll be fine."

He helped her stand, then walked her the few feet to the car. Soon they were heading back to Jarrod Ridge.

"How do you feel now?" he said a few minutes later.

"Okay."

They drove a little farther. "Talk to me, Samantha."

"I don't really feel like talking," she said, calling herself an idiot for slipping. If only she'd looked where she was going, then—

"I want you to stay awake. You may have a slight concussion."

"Oh." She realized this was the correct procedure.

"Come on, you can do better than that," he said, a serious look in his eyes.

"Okay." She tried to think. "What do you want me to say?"

"I don't know. Anything. What's your favorite color?"

She didn't need to think about that. "Yellow."

His brow rose in surprise. "Yellow? Any particular reason?"

She winced a little as she adjusted the woolen hat against the injury. "Because it's bright and happy."

He glanced at her again, noting her wince, his mouth turning grim. "Okay, so what's your favorite flower?"

"Tulips."

Another look of surprise from him. "Why?"

"They're so beautiful."

There was a tiny pause. "Like you," he murmured, and her breath caught, then she moved her head and winced again. "Not long now," he assured her.

After that Blake drove straight up to the clinic at the spa lodge. The middle-aged nurse immediately took control, putting Samantha in an exam room. She checked her over, mentioning it wasn't too bad but that she'd need to call the doctor anyway.

"No need to get Joel if he's busy," Samantha said, feeling bad for interrupting his Sunday morning.

Blake nodded at the nurse. "Get him."

The nurse nodded in agreement then looked at her. "The doctor really should see you," she said, then went and picked up the wall telephone as Samantha glanced at Blake.

He gave a short shake of his head. "He's paid to do his job, Samantha. Let him."

Before too long, Joel strode into the exam room, nodding at Blake and giving her a chiding frown. "What have you done to yourself, Sam?"

Samantha didn't look at Blake, but she sensed he'd noted the shortening of her name. Joel was professional in his examination. She didn't need stitches but he tidied up the cut and it finally stopped bleeding. Thankfully he hadn't needed to cut any of her hair in the process.

"I don't think the lump on your head is anything to be concerned about," he assured her, "but we still need to keep an eye on it for any signs of concussion." He considered her. "If you like, I can come to Pine Lodge and check on you a couple of times throughout the day."

"I'll take care of her," Blake said firmly. "I know what signs to look for."

Joel glanced at Blake, held his gaze a moment, then nodded. "Fine. But I'll drop by the lodge and check on her this evening. Call me sooner if you have any doubts."

"I will."

Samantha looked from one to the other. "Do either of you mind if I have a say in this?"

Blake shot her an impatient look, but it was Joel who spoke. "Sam, this has to be taken very seriously. Your brain's had a knock, and sometimes things can develop later on. You need to rest up and you need to have someone keep a close eye on you for at least twenty-four hours."

She swallowed, not sure she liked hearing that, but before she could say anything the clinic door opened and someone called out for help, saying something about a twisted ankle. The nurse and Joel excused themselves to go check.

Blake came to stand in front of her. "I intend to look after you whether you like it or not."

"But—"

"It's my fault you were out there today," he cut across her, his eyes holding firm regret. "No arguments, Samantha. I owe you this."

She melted faster than snow under a heat lamp. "All right."

There was nothing in his eyes that said he remembered their kiss, and right now she was grateful for that. She would have plenty of time to go over it once she was alone.

He picked up her jacket. "Come on, then," he said gruffly. "Let's get this on you and get you back home."

Home?

Why did that sound so good to her?

Five

By the time Blake brought her back to Pine Lodge it was almost noon. Not that Samantha was hungry. She wasn't. She was glad now that he'd decided to stay close today. She wasn't feeling ill, but she was still a little shaky, so she was appreciative of him cupping her elbow as they walked.

That shakiness increased as they went up the staircase and he told her that tonight she was to sleep in the spare bedroom in his suite—a spare bedroom separated from his bedroom by only a connecting bathroom.

Her stomach dipped as they reached the top stair. "I'm only across the landing there, Blake. It seems silly not to stay in my own room."

"No. I want you near in case you need me."

She *did* need him, but not in the way he meant. He was being nothing more than caring right now, while she was still stunned by the impact of their kiss back on the mountain.

"Fine," she murmured, not up to arguing anyway. She was a bit of a mess. Her jacket had mud on it, her slacks were still slightly damp in places where she'd fallen on the wet grass, and parts of her brown hair felt like it was matted with blood. Yuk! She must look a wonderful sight.

"I need to change my clothes," she said, wrinkling her nose. "Actually I might have a shower. My hair feels sticky."

He shook his head. "Not a good idea. You might faint in there."

Her heart thudded and she could feel her face heat up as she pictured him coming in to rescue her. She looked away as they walked toward her room. "You're right," she said, then could have kicked herself. Any other woman would have used that to her advantage, but no, not her. What was the matter with her? Then she remembered. That's right, she'd had a bump on the head, she excused herself, wincing.

"Are you in pain?"

"A little."

He pushed open her bedroom door and led her inside. "Here. Sit on the chair and let me help you take off your jacket."

"Thanks." She did as he said.

"Your sweater's got dried blood down the back of it," he said, after he'd eased her out of the padded material. "I don't know how you're going to get it over your head without causing pain." A small pause. "I'll have to help you off with it."

She gulped. "You will?"

"Yes." His voice was nothing but neutral.

She tried to appear nonchalant, too. "Trust me to wear a tight-necked sweater today," she joked, feeling dizzy again but not from her injuries. It was the thought of him undressing her, even though it made sense to do it this way. She didn't think she'd be able to get the sweater off without him. She had a long-sleeved T-shirt underneath to cover herself, but that had a wide neck and she could easily take it off herself.

"Right. This won't take long." His voice sounded tight and she wondered... "Keep still now."

He slid her arms out of the sleeves, then she felt him touch the hem of her sweater, and almost like it was in slow motion he started to lift it upward. She could feel him move close...closer still as he inched it up higher and higher.... She could feel his breath change as he neared her breasts, though not once did he touch her in any intimate way.

"Okay, careful now," he said, as he reached her nape, his voice huskier. "This will be a little tricky." He moved closer.... "There. That's it. Now let me ease it over your head." He moved around to the front of her and eased the knit material gently up over her head, and suddenly it was off and she was sitting there, her gaze level with his belt buckle. And then she raised her eyes to his, saw him looking down at her, and she dropped her eyes to where her T-shirt had ridden up and was revealing her breasts cupped in her lacy blue bra.

She lifted her head again and their eyes locked together. Something dark flared in his, and in retaliation her breathing became practically nonexistent as she remembered their kiss. Until that moment back there on the mountain none of this had been purely about *them*.

Things had changed.

Now it was.

All at once he twisted jerkily toward the small table and placed the sweater on it, saying over his shoulder, "I'll leave you to do the rest, but I'll be back soon to check on you." His voice sounded rough as he headed for the door. "You should get into bed."

She realized he was trying to be a gentleman and keep it all under control because she was injured, but what if she wasn't injured? Would he take her?

The thought was moot, she told herself, swallowing hard and concentrating on what he'd said. "I'm not staying up here all day, Blake. I can sit on the couch downstairs and do some work." It didn't feel right to go to bed in the middle of the day. Not unless…

He stopped at the door, his eyes firm. "I won't let you work, but you can lie on the couch."

"Good of you," she joked, trying to ease the tension in the room.

He didn't smile. He had a hard flush on his face. "I think so," he muttered, then left her to it, shutting the door behind him and giving her some privacy.

Swallowing, she had to move or he might come back and decide to help her undress the rest of her clothes. And that wouldn't be such a bad thing on her part, but clearly he didn't want to right now. She appreciated that he was thinking of her, even as her body craved to be a part of his.

First, she went into her bathroom, groaning when she saw a streak of blood on her cheek and the mess of her hair. Carefully she lifted the T-shirt over her head.

Unable to stop herself, she stared at her lace-clad breasts, her cheeks reddening as she thought of Blake seeing the invitation of her body like this.

Filling the sink with warm water, she grabbed a washcloth and cleaned as much of the blood out of her hair as possible, then very gently combed it into place over the cut. She was pleased with the result. If she didn't know better, and if her head hadn't been sore, it would be hard to believe she'd just had an accident.

But if she was going to be an invalid today, she may as well be comfortable. She changed into denim jeans and a long-sleeve blouse that buttoned up so she didn't have to lift it over her head. Blake tapped on the door as she stepped into a pair of slides.

"Come in," she called out, half-surprised he'd knocked, considering he'd appeared to have taken charge of her welfare.

He pushed open the door then stood there, inspecting her from the face up. "You look much better."

"I feel better. Thanks."

Then his gaze traveled downward and a curious look passed over his face. "I don't remember seeing you in jeans before."

One glance from him and she could feel how much the jeans hugged her figure. Her stomach fluttered. "I usually only wear them at home." If they were staying at a hotel, Pine Lodge included, she wore stylish clothes even when going casual. She considered dressing right a part of her job.

"You should wear them more often," he said, his eyes blank but his voice tight again. He stepped back. "Come on. There's a couch waiting for you downstairs."

She avoided his gaze as she walked forward, then

went past him in the doorway, but she could feel his presence like a soft touch.

Thankfully soon she was lying on the couch with cushions behind her back and a throw over her body. Did she want a book to read, he asked. A movie on the DVD player? A magazine?

"Perhaps some magazines," she said, though she didn't actually feel like doing anything but lying there and being with Blake. "You don't have to do this," she said as he went to get them from the rack.

He came back with a selection, his mouth set. "I told you. It's my fault you were injured in the first place. I shouldn't have taken you with me."

"But you were only wanting to show me the bungalow location before I left Aspen," she said in a flood of words, then saw his mouth tighten further. She understood. She didn't want to be reminded that she was leaving soon either. "Anyway, what's done is done. I don't blame you but if you want to make it up to me, then I'd love a hot drink. A hot chocolate would be nice. With marshmallows."

"No."

She blinked. "Why not?"

"Because you shouldn't be drinking or eating for a few hours. It could make things worse."

She realized he was right, but, "I'm really thirsty, Blake, and I'm feeling fine now. How about some peppermint tea? That shouldn't hurt." She watched him consider that.

He nodded grudgingly. "Only a very weak one, then."

She smiled. "Thanks."

He set off for the kitchen and she could hear him

moving about in there. Her family used to cosset her like this at times, and she had to admit she liked being taken care of by Blake.

He soon returned with her hot drink, then he moved to the table in the corner where they'd set up the office. For a time it remained quiet as she flipped through the magazines and sipped at her tea. Then she began feeling sleepy. Eventually she finished her drink and made herself more comfortable, being careful with her sore head as she curled up on the couch. Her eyes closed and she found herself thinking about her and Blake back on the mountain. She could still remember the feel of his lips against...

The phone woke her with a start and she heard Blake swearing as he snatched it from the handset. She sat up and tidied herself, listening to his conversation, knowing someone in his family was inquiring about her. He soon ended the call.

"Sorry about that," he told her. "It was Guy checking to see how you were. He'd heard about the accident from Avery."

"Oh, that's nice of him."

The phone rang again and Blake reached for it. "Yes, she's fine, Gavin, but I'll be keeping an eye on her anyway." She saw Blake listen, then dart a look at her, before turning away. "You're a funny guy, Gav." Then he hung up.

Curious, she asked, "What did he say?"

"Nothing much."

Had Gavin made a brotherly comment about keeping an eye on her? Not that she minded. It might work in her favor. "That's good of your family to be checking on me."

"You're supposed to be resting. I don't want them interrupting that."

His comment warmed her as she glanced at the wall clock, surprised to see the time. "I must have been asleep a while."

"An hour."

So he'd been keeping an eye on her. "That long? I didn't realize."

"I did."

The phone rang again and he muttered something low. This time it was Trevor. No sooner had he hung up than they heard car doors slam shut and Blake strode over to look out the window.

"Who is it?" she asked.

"Melissa and Shane."

She watched him start toward the front door and quickly called his name. He stopped to look at her. "You *will* let them in, won't you?"

His mouth tightened. "For a short while."

"Be nice," she chided gently, and he shot her a look saying that was a given. "You know what I mean, Blake. I think it's wonderful of your family to be concerned for me."

His mouth softened a little. "Yeah, they're pretty good when they want to be."

Soon Blake's sister Melissa and her new fiancé, Shane McDermott, came into the lodge, bringing a breath of crisp, fresh air.

Melissa's long, wavy, blond hair flew behind her as she made a beeline for the couch. "Samantha! We heard you'd had an accident. Are you okay?"

Samantha was touched that they'd thought to drop by. "I'm fine, Melissa. Thank you for thinking of me."

"She's fine for the moment," Blake said, standing closest to the door, as if ready to open it in a moment's notice. "But she needs to rest as much as possible."

Shane stood beside him but he at least smiled at her, unlike Blake. "Good to see you, Samantha," he said, inclining his head in the cowboy way.

Samantha smiled back at the handsome man. Shane was the architect who'd designed the resort's riding stables. He might look urban and sophisticated, but he'd been raised on a nearby ranch and his cowboy status couldn't be disputed. "You, too, Shane."

Melissa sank down on one of the lounge chairs and frowned at Samantha. "You do look pale. So tell me. What happened?" Without giving her time to reply, she glanced at the men. "Blake, I'd love a hot chocolate so be a dear and make me one, won't you?" She darted a look at Samantha. "What about you, honey?"

Samantha wrinkled her nose. "Blake won't let me."

Melissa seemed to consider that, then darted a look at her brother before nodding at Samantha. "Yes, that's probably best." She looked at her fiancé. "Shane, darling, would you mind helping Blake in the kitchen? I'm not sure he knows his way around it," she teased.

Blake eased into his first smile since they'd arrived. "You'd be surprised, Melissa."

Melissa patted the small hump of her stomach on her slightly curvy figure. "You'd better hurry. This baby is getting hungry." She winked at Samantha.

Samantha smiled but as the men left them alone and she looked at Blake's sister, she felt a tug deep inside her chest. Melissa had a radiant glow about her. She'd only recently announced her pregnancy to Shane and they were soon to be married. They'd had a few ups and downs but now all was well.

Samantha was very happy for Melissa, and yet she felt sad for herself, with this inexplicable ache in the region of her heart. One day she wanted a baby and a family of her own, but she couldn't imagine any man she wanted to father them—except for maybe Blake. That would mean he would have to marry her, but he didn't believe in happily-ever-after, and she wasn't ready for that either.

Still, she couldn't shake off the thought of cuddling Blake's baby in her arms. It was natural for a woman to think about having children with the man she was attracted to, right? Strangely, she didn't ever remember thinking about having Carl's children. Her notion of being married to him had merely been about them traveling the world together. It hadn't progressed further than that. Thank the Lord!

"Are you okay, Samantha?"

She managed a smile. "Apart from a small headache, I'm fine."

Melissa's piercing blue eyes suddenly seemed so like Blake's. "I hear you're leaving us soon?"

This was why the other woman had got the men out of the way. Melissa wanted to question her.

Samantha tried to look at peace with her decision. "Yes, it's time to move on to new pastures."

"Blake will miss you."

"So everyone keeps telling me," Samantha said wryly, but was grateful that Shane came back in right then to ask Melissa a question about how hot she wanted her drink. Once he left again Samantha changed the conversation to the ranch where Shane had grown up. Melissa was more than happy to talk about her fiancé.

The other couple stayed for a while, until Blake shooed them out, reminding them that a certain person needed to rest up.

"Right," Blake said, once they'd gone. "I'll get some more work out of the way, then how does an omelet sound for dinner? I don't think you should eat anything too heavy, just in case. It's not a good thing to have a full stomach."

She looked at him in mild amusement. "Is this Doctor Jarrod speaking?"

He didn't seem to find that funny. "Yes, so take note."

"I would, only you won't let me work," she quipped.

"Funny," he muttered, then went back to his paperwork. She sighed. He was taking it all so seriously, and while that was sweet of him, it wasn't necessary.

After that, Samantha was itching to get up and move around but knew it was best she take things easy. For something to do while she was waiting for Blake to finish working, she popped a movie in the DVD and began watching it with earphones so that she didn't disturb him. It was a romantic comedy she hadn't seen before and it made her giggle. She didn't realize she'd been laughing loudly until suddenly she became aware of Blake standing near the couch.

She paused the movie and looked up at him as she pulled out her earbuds. "I'm sorry. Is this interrupting your work?"

"No." He went still. "It's good to hear you laugh. You don't do it often enough."

Her pulse was skipping beats. "The job isn't exactly a laugh a minute," she joked. Then realized how that might sound. "That came out wrong. I didn't mean—"

"I know what you meant," he said easily enough as he leaned over and pulled the earplug cord out of the television. Picking up the remote, he turned the movie back on, only instead of going back to his work he sat down on the other chair.

She blinked in mild surprise, then tried to concentrate as he began watching the movie with her. He'd only missed about fifteen minutes of the story, so they both watched it together. It was amusing enough that she could feel herself relax, and when it was finished even Blake looked relaxed. She was glad about that. He worked too hard at times, and took his responsibilities too seriously.

Later, in spite of him telling her to stay on the couch, she followed him into the kitchen where he was going to prepare dinner. "I need to walk. My legs are getting numb."

His brows immediately drew together on full medical alert. "They feel numb? Are you getting any pins and needles? Is it hard to walk or are—"

"Blake, I was merely trying to say I wanted to move around," she cut across him, somewhat bemused by his agitation.

He grimaced. "Okay, so that was a mild over-reaction."

"Mild?" she teased.

He gave a self-deprecating smile, then jerked his head toward the bench. "Go sit over there and take it easy."

She ignored that and turned toward the cupboard.

"I'll put out the place mats and cutlery first. We can eat in here."

He must have known it was a waste of time to argue because he nodded, then went back to preparing the omelet. It was a strange feeling watching him cook for her. It would be another memory to take away when she left.

Soon they were sitting down on the tall stools to eat and the next hour flew by as they chatted. As if they both didn't want to ruin the moment, neither of them spoke about her leaving.

Then he mentioned Donald Jarrod in passing, and that made her think. Blake had never spoken about his father while they were in Vegas, but now they were in Aspen she'd managed to put two and two together. "Your dad was pretty hard on you, wasn't he?"

He tensed even as he gave a light shrug. "After my mother died, he was hard on all his children."

She considered him. "But harder on you."

A flash of surprise crossed his face. "Yes. How did you know?"

"You were the eldest. He seems to have been a man who had set ideas about the order of things and didn't give an inch."

"He was. Very much so."

"Tell me more."

He paused and for a moment she didn't think he would tell her. Then, "Guy was only younger by a few minutes but it could have been years in my father's eyes. I was the oldest, so it was up to me to make sure I took responsibility for everything. None of us ever really got to play while growing up, but I suppose I got even less time than the rest."

The thought upset her. "That's sad."

He shrugged. "My father actually did us a favor. We grew up being very independent. We don't need anyone."

She could see that. And that was even sadder, but she didn't say so. She tilted her head. "It still would've been hard losing your mother like that when you were just a small boy. And then having your father distance himself would have made it far worse. Children don't understand why love has been withdrawn. They just know."

His expression suddenly bordered on mockery and she knew she'd touched a nerve. "And you understand the way a child's mind works when he loses a parent, do you?"

She pulled a face. He knew very well both her parents were alive. "Well, no, but—"

"I rest my case."

"Blake, I don't think it's too hard to comprehend what you must have gone through."

Anger flashed across his face. "Enough, Samantha. I don't want or need your sympathy for something that happened a long time ago."

"But—"

The telephone rang and he snatched it up from the wall beside him, almost barking into it. His mouth tightened. "Hang on, Erica. I'll put her on." He handed the phone over to Samantha.

"I see Blake's being his usual talkative self," Erica mused down the line. She didn't wait for Samantha to agree. "I heard about your accident and just wanted to see how you were doing."

Samantha appreciated her concern. "I'm fine, thanks,

Erica." She forced herself to sound cheery. "Blake and I just had dinner. He cooked me an omelet."

An eloquent silence came from Erica's end. "A man of many talents," she finally said. "I'd better let you go, then. I'll talk to you tomorrow." She hung up before Samantha could respond.

Samantha took her time placing the receiver back down, hiding her expression from him. She wouldn't tell Blake what Erica had been thinking. That his half sister was delighted the two of them were bonding, even if Blake did sound like a grouch. "That was really nice of her to call."

His lips twisted. "I wonder if I have any relatives left who might like to interrupt us tonight?"

Her brow creased with worry. "You really should give Erica a chance."

"To do what?"

Anger stirred the air, though she knew it wasn't directed at her. She tilted her head. "Do you blame Erica for your father's affair with her mother?" she said, coming right out and saying it.

He didn't look pleased by her comment. "I'm not blaming Erica for what my father did. I just don't want her coming in here and splitting up the family. I'm not convinced she'll stay in Aspen."

She didn't know how he could say that. Was he blind? "She and Christian are so in love. And she's in love with everyone here at Jarrod Ridge, too. Their hearts are here, Blake. They won't leave you."

He swore. "I don't give a rat's ass if they leave or not. This isn't about what *I* feel anyway. It's about her causing problems for the family and then walking away without a care in the world."

"I'm sure that won't happen. Erica isn't like that."

One eyebrow shot up. "You know her so well, do you?"

"Do you?"

A muscle began ticking along his jaw. "Thank you for your opinion, but I don't need it." He pushed to his feet and began collecting the plates, taking them over to the dishwasher. "Go into the living room. I'll bring in the coffee."

For a few moments she didn't move. She watched his rigid back and felt depressed by his remoteness and abruptness. She'd pushed him hard just now and she wasn't sure why, except that she somehow felt she was fighting not just for Erica's sake but for Blake's, as well. If she could at least get him to relent toward Erica then maybe when *she* left, her time here would have been of value. Maybe then something good would have come from all this. She sighed. Or was she simply looking for something to make herself feel good about leaving Blake?

And that brought her back to what she'd said before about Erica leaving him. Was that the crux of the matter? It occurred to her then that Blake may have abandonment issues with his mother dying, and now that made it difficult for him to get close to his half sister. Or to get close to anyone, including herself.

Someone rang the doorbell and Blake swore again.

"That'll be Joel," Samantha reminded him. "He said he would check on me."

"Stay there," he muttered and strode past her to let in the other man.

A couple of seconds later Joel breezed into the kitchen. She noticed he took in the homey scene, but he was all professional while he checked her over and announced he was pleased.

Then, "We have to get you better for tomorrow night," he teased, but she saw him dart a look at Blake and she suddenly had the feeling there was more to this. He seemed to be letting Blake know he was staking a claim.

"Tomorrow night?" Blake asked in a menacing voice.

Joel closed up his medical bag. "Samantha and I have a date for Monday night." He winked at her. "We're going to the movies."

Samantha wanted to say she hadn't actually accepted the invitation but the displeased look in Blake's eyes kept her quiet.

"Let's see how she feels first," Blake said grimly, then stepped back in clear indication that the doctor should precede him to the front door.

Joel hesitated, like he wasn't about to take orders, then he must have remembered that Blake was his boss. He inclined his head at Samantha. "I'll call you in the morning," he told her, picking up his bag.

He left the room and Blake saw him out, and Samantha couldn't help but wonder once again if Blake might be jealous of Joel. The thought made her heartbeat pick up speed. Blake had certainly *wanted* to kiss her back there on the mountain and surely that had to mean something.

Didn't it?

All at once she needed to know what he felt for her. "Joel finds me attractive, don't you think?" she said dreamily as Blake came back in the kitchen looking anything but relaxed.

His eyes filled with meaning. "Sure he does," he said cynically.

She couldn't let him get away with that. "What does that mean?"

"Just that any woman with the right equipment can attract a man. And believe me, you've got the right equipment," he drawled, slipping his hands into his trouser pockets, all at once looking very much in charge of himself, making her want to bring him down a peg or two.

"Thanks for the assumption that I'm only good for sex," she said with faint indignation.

His hands came out of his pockets and his complacency vanished. "I didn't say that," he retorted, then strode over to check on the coffee. He spun back around. "Dammit, what the hell are you doing with those men anyway? You don't need them. They're beneath you."

Startled, she gathered her wits about her. *This* was more like it. "Maybe I *want* them beneath me," she joked.

"Don't talk like that."

She hid a soft gasp. It *did* sound like he was jealous. She needed to push more. "I don't understand how you can say a doctor isn't good enough for me, Blake."

"That's because he's *not* good enough for you."

Her spirits soared. "What about Ralph? You don't even know what he does for a living."

"And you do?"

She did, then realized she'd set herself up here. She had to cough before she said, "He's a car salesman."

"Huh! That explains the slime rolling off him."

"Blake!" She hadn't expected quite such a response. "What's got into you?"

His mouth drew down at the corners. "Those guys aren't after you for your intellect."

She screwed up her nose. "How nice of you to point that out."

"You know what I'm saying."

Yes, she did. Unfortunately she knew it was true. And that would have been fine if she'd been the least bit interested in the other men. As it was, she still felt a little guilty using them, though no doubt they were big enough to look out for themselves.

She tilted her head and knew she had to say this. "If I didn't know better I'd think you were jealous."

"And if I am?" he challenged without warning.

She felt giddy but she couldn't let herself get her hopes up. "I'd have to ask why. Is it because you know I'm leaving soon and you only want what you suddenly can't have?"

"What the—"

"Or is it because you might actually want *me?*"

For a moment he looked like he would move in close. "You ask me that after the kiss we shared?"

Her breath came quickly. "I—"

And then something changed in his expression and his jaw thrust forward. "This isn't the time to discuss it. You need your rest. You should go lie on the couch."

Her throat blocked with disappointment, but then understanding dawned and she realized he was pulling back for *her* sake. If it hadn't been for her accident, she was sure he would be making love to her right now.

Frustration weaved through her, despite appreciating that he was doing the right thing. "I think I'll go read in bed. It's getting late." He went to come with her and she put her hand up. "No, I can manage by myself. Good night, Blake. And thanks."

He nodded. "Make sure you sleep in the spare bedroom. I still want you close to me."

She could feel heat sweeping up her face. Did he have to say it like that? "Okay."

He seemed mesmerized by her reddening cheeks. "I'll be checking on you a couple of times in the night." His voice had a gravelly edge to it now. "So I apologize in advance for disturbing you."

She looked away; the thought of him coming into her room during the night was enough to disturb her *now*.

Then she went up to bed with stars in her eyes. And they weren't from the hit on the head either. Unfortunately she knew he wasn't about to take advantage of her while she was injured, and certainly not during the night when she was sure he'd remain a perfect gentleman. But he'd better watch out when she was back on her feet.

Six

Blake looked at the bedside clock and grunted to himself. It was almost seven o'clock and still dark outside, but he needed to get up and check on Samantha before he did anything else this morning. Today he planned on working from Pine Lodge so he could keep an eye on her, but he needed to go to the Manor and get some things out of the way first.

He'd spent a restless night, getting up every couple of hours to check on a sleeping Samantha in the bedroom next door. Of course it was easy for her to sleep so peacefully. She didn't have to stand over an attractive member of the opposite sex who wore satin pajamas and looked deliciously alluring in bed. And she didn't have to reach out to touch that person's shoulder to shake them awake, nor rigidly ignore the urge to slide into bed next to her warm body and pleasure her senseless.

He would have done it, too—if he hadn't had to

wake her and ask questions to make sure she wasn't suffering any sort of confusion. Even now the thought of her having any sort of aftereffects from the head injury still managed to clench his gut tight. He'd hated seeing her hurt. If he hadn't been so focused on getting her away from that Ralph, then none of this would have happened.

Not even the kiss.

No, that kiss *would* have happened—if not there, then somewhere else. There was something going on between them now. It had started happening the night she'd handed him her resignation and it hadn't let up.

And it wasn't one-sided either. She'd dissolved in his arms so quickly yesterday he'd thought the marrow had melted in her bones. No woman had ever reacted quite like that for him before. It certainly made a man feel good.

Remembering the feel of her lips beneath his, he was tempted to just lie there and think about her, but he knew he'd never get out of bed if he did. And then Samantha would be bringing *him* breakfast in bed. The thought was more than pleasurable.

Giving a low groan, he tossed back the covers and shoved off the mattress in his pajama bottoms, then headed for the bathroom to take a shower. But as he opened the door and went to reach for the light switch, the light flicked on anyway and Samantha came through the connecting door.

She jumped back with a gasp. "Blake!"

A lick of fire sizzled through his veins as his eyes slid down over her slim contours, registering that what he thought had been green satin pajamas was an emerald midthigh nightshirt. It looked so sexy on her, suiting her complexion and rich brown hair.

He lifted his eyes back up to her face. "How's the head?" he asked huskily.

She seemed to become flustered. "Er…it doesn't feel too bad." Awkwardly she spun to face the mirrored wall, going up on her toes to stare at her reflection. "I came to see if it was okay." She lifted her long tousled strands to check the injury. "Yes, it looks fine," she chattered. "There's a bit of a bump and no sign of bleeding."

He appreciated that she was okay, but did she know that stretching up over the sink like she was, the side split of her nightshirt was showing him more of her long silken legs than he'd ever seen before? All the way up her thigh to the line of her panties.

Suddenly she seemed to freeze in position as she stretched up at the mirror like that, and he realized right then she was looking at *him* in the mirror, with a hungry look that drifted down over his bare chest and the pajama bottoms he'd worn last night for her benefit. He tensed with arousal and she must have noticed. Their eyes locked together in the glass.

And then she slowly pushed back from the sink and turned to face him with her body, her chin tilting provocatively, her eyes inviting him to take her. Caught off-guard by such an unfamiliar look from her, he swallowed hard. His assistant was certainly showing him a new side of herself lately.

"Samantha," he said thickly, galvanized into taking a step toward her. "Do you know what you're—"

"Yes, Blake, I do."

He reached her and she tumbled against him, her hands flattening against his chest, her mouth seeking his, her lips parting beneath his without any pressure at all.

Their kiss was hot and urgent and demanding, their bodies pressing closer and closer together, reveling in each other. Then a soft moan of hers breathed into him, and in a haze of desire, he deepened the kiss until he finally had to break away to suck in air.

But only for a moment, until he began planting quick, soft kisses down that creamy throat, before coming back up again to her lips, needing to be inside her mouth once more, needing to breathe her in once more.

He pulled her harder against him, running his hands hungrily over the satin material and feminine curves. She quivered all over from head to toe, wildly gripping his shoulders like she needed to hold on to him.

Mouth to mouth, he backed her to the full-length sink and lifted her up onto a folded fluffy towel. Her thighs fell open and he heard a button pop from the front of her nightshirt. He gave a groan of approval and wedged himself between her legs….

And the coldness of the marble touched his erection through his pajamas.

The shock of it made him still. Heaven knew he could do with cooling down…slowing down…but Samantha sat in front of him with her head tilted back and her eyes closed. Her cheeks were overheated, her breathing unsteady, and despite that come-to-me look she'd given him a short while ago, she appeared to be about to lose control. God knows he'd felt the instantaneous spiral of desire himself, but this was more and he really had to wonder just how inexperienced she actually was. He swallowed hard. Could she even be a *virgin?*

He wasn't sure how he felt about that, but he did

know he couldn't continue this right now. His previous lovers knew the score but this woman may not. And if he was playing with more than her body…if her emotions were more than involved…he could cause her a lot of heartache. He didn't want to do that to Samantha.

Yet this wasn't the moment to talk about it, with her looking all sexy and ready for the taking. There was too much hunger in the air in here. It would only confuse things. He liked her too much to do this to her.

Unwrapping her arms from around his neck, he lifted her down off the bench, hating that he had to walk away from her. "I'm sorry, Samantha."

Bewilderment spread over her face. "What's the—"

"I just can't do it," he rasped. "Not like this." As hard as it was to leave her side, he turned and went back to his room.

He badly wanted to turn right back around, sweep her up in his arms and carry her to his bed. He shuddered as he closed the door between them.

They would talk later and perhaps it would turn out that he'd have to keep the door closed permanently between them. Maybe she would be his road not taken. But he had to think what was best for Samantha. She deserved better than becoming his temporary mistress.

Samantha didn't know how she made it back to her own room. Humiliation scorched through her. She'd done exactly what she'd wanted to do and given Blake a come-on. She hadn't deliberately gone into the bathroom to entice him in there, but the opportunity had presented itself and she'd thought it had worked. Then he'd just upped and walked away and, despite his obvious arousal, he said he couldn't do it.

Couldn't make love with her.

She knew it had nothing to do with her having a minor head injury this time. He might say it was, but she knew this was about him not wanting her enough. His body had automatically responded to a female in his arms, but his mind had been elsewhere. As he'd said the evening before, any woman with the right equipment could attract a man. Unfortunately the attraction he felt for her hadn't been enough. Not for him.

It was Carl all over again.

She plopped down on her bed as her legs gave way. Had she unwittingly done something wrong back there? Something to annoy him physically? Clearly he hadn't been invested in the moment like she'd been. It had been wonderful in his arms but she hadn't realized he'd been feeling different. She thought he'd felt the same way. It was obvious now that he could turn himself on and off at a whim—just like he had after their kiss on the mountain.

Unlike her.

Her emotions whirled like a spinning top let loose on the floor. Oh, God, what was she going to do? How was she going to face him? Worse, would he insist on letting her out of her contract now? She had the feeling he would tell her to leave sooner rather than later.

At the thought, her emotions stopped spinning. They stopped dead. Her chin lifted. Right. Okay. If she was being given the heave-ho, then she would certainly leave without protest. It's what she needed to do anyway, she told herself. She regretted she would leave with this between them, but things had gone too far. It was a good lesson in being careful what she wished for. Now she simply wished this nightmare would go away.

Samantha took a shower and carefully washed her hair, but wasn't sure if she was dismayed or relieved after she came out of the bathroom and heard Blake's car leaving. Going over to peek out her bedroom window, she saw him driving toward the Manor in the early morning light. Evidently she was okay to be left alone now, she thought with a stab of hurt.

Then her heart dropped to her feet. Perhaps he was going to tell his family that she was leaving sooner? Would he tell them why? That she'd made a play for him and put him in an awkward position? Her cheeks heated at the thought and she wanted to curl up in a ball and not see any of them again.

Yet pride wouldn't allow her to do that. She'd held her head high when Carl had rejected her and she would do it again now. She would go up to the Manor and finish her tasks, and she would arrange her replacement. If she smiled at the others and acted carefree, then no one would know how bad she felt.

No one except Blake.

Half an hour later she sat at her desk at the Manor, relieved not to have seen anyone she knew on the way here. She didn't want to answer questions about her accident, or anything else for that matter.

Thankfully the door to Blake's office was shut, though the red light on the telephone told her he was making a call. Quickly she got herself organized, then found the number she was after and reached for the phone, hoping someone at the employment agency would be at their desk early like her. She knew that as soon as the red button on his phone lit up with her extension, Blake would learn she was here, but it couldn't be helped.

She got the answering machine. Having dealt with this employment agency before for other office matters, she decided to leave a message. At least that would get the ball rolling. "Yes, this is Samantha Thompson calling on behalf of Blake Jarrod Enterprises. Could Mary Wentworth call me back as soon as possible…" The red light on Blake's phone went off. Her heart started to race as a second later his door was flung open. "It's about a position that's become available." He strode to her desk. "It's—"

He pressed the button to disconnect the call, his eyes slamming into her. "What are you doing?" he demanded in a low tone.

She angled her chin as she looked up at him. "I'm trying to work."

"I thought you'd have enough sense to rest up today."

"I don't need to rest up. I did plenty of that yesterday." Calmly, she placed the telephone back on its handset. "I'm perfectly fine now."

His eyes narrowed. "And why the hell are you calling someone about your job?"

"You need a new assistant."

"I'm happy with my old one."

She arched one eyebrow. "Really? It didn't seem that way to me this morning," she said, staying cool when all she wanted to do was fall in a heap and cry her eyes out.

He swore.

"Don't worry, Blake. I'll be leaving Aspen soon, so

you don't have to worry that I'll attack you. I know you're not that into me."

He blinked, then, "What the hell!" He swore again. "We need to talk."

"It's a bit late for talking, don't you think?" She went to pick up the phone again. He grabbed her hand, not hurting her but not letting her make the call either. "Stop manhandling me, Blake."

He tried to stare her down. "No."

"Blake, this isn't getting us anywhere."

"Listen, Samantha. You're—"

Erica walked into the office and stopped dead, blinking in surprise as her gaze went from one to the other, then down at their hands gripped together. "Er... Blake, your car is here to take you to the airport."

He casually let go of Samantha's hand. "Thanks, Erica."

Samantha felt the blood drain from her face. "You're leaving?"

Like Carl?

He looked at her oddly. "Something cropped up overnight at one of the hotels and I need to go to Vegas and sort it out. I'll tell you about it later."

As fast as it had tightened, the tension unscrewed inside her. So he *was* coming back. It had been crazy of her to even think he wouldn't. Blake wouldn't give up all this because of *her*.

She went to get to her feet. "I'll come with you." Once she was in Vegas, she would start bringing her life there to a close.

"No, you stay here. You shouldn't be flying with a head injury," he said firmly, surprising her. She'd have thought he'd be eager to get her out of Aspen now.

He cast his half sister a look. "Erica, can you keep an eye on Samantha and make sure she doesn't stay here too long today? I don't want her overdoing things."

Erica looked startled then pleased. "Of course." It was obvious she valued being asked by her brother to help out, but Samantha was still surprised that Blake wanted *her* to stay in Aspen.

He nodded. "Thanks. I'll just grab my stuff." As he spoke he headed back into his office before coming out with his briefcase and coat. He looked at Samantha. "I'll be back tonight. I'll explain everything then." He started toward the door then hesitated. "You *will* be here when I return, won't you, Samantha?"

It hadn't occurred to her to leave behind his back, though she couldn't discount that it might have. Then she remembered how she'd thought he might have issues with feeling abandoned over his mother's death. Did he think *she* was about to abandon him, too? Tenderness touched a part of her that wasn't reeling by the latest events. "I promise."

He looked satisfied then he gave Erica a jerky nod as he passed by. He left behind a meaningful silence.

After a couple of seconds, Erica came toward the desk. "Are you okay?"

"My head's fine now, thanks."

She tutted. "You know I mean more than that."

Samantha grimaced. "Yes, I suppose I do." Then as she looked at the other woman, she wondered if Blake would eventually discuss her with his family. Would he even tell them she had made a play for him? Her breath caught. She'd never known him to talk about his affairs before to anyone. Huh! Affair? There *was* no affair. That was the problem.

"He's concerned for you, honey."

"He's concerned for the job."

"You're wrong." Erica paused. "Give him a chance to explain whatever it is he needs to explain."

The telephone rang then, and Erica said she had to go check on something but would be back later. Samantha answered it and heard Mary Wentworth's voice, and knew she needed to slow everything down a little. So she apologized to the other woman that she couldn't talk right now and would call her back tomorrow. By then, she should well and truly know the score between her and Blake. Either way, she still had to leave. It was just a matter of when.

After she hung up, the workday began with the phone ringing, then the mail arrived. Samantha worked through it all, but a part of her mind was on Blake's reaction earlier. He'd said he was perfectly happy with his old assistant.

Her.

And that made her wonder if he might still want her to work out her contract. Her heart raced at the thought, then came to a shuddering halt when she remembered this morning in the bathroom. She probably couldn't stay at Jarrod Ridge past tomorrow, but at least on his return tonight she might learn what had turned him off her. It may not be something she wanted to hear, but she needed to know or she would always wonder.

Erica returned an hour later, but Samantha still felt physically fine and convinced her not to worry. She'd decided to work until lunchtime, then she got a ride back to the lodge, where she made herself a light lunch. Afterward she felt tired, so she stretched out on the couch and took a nap.

The front doorbell woke her sometime later. It was a florist with a vase filled with the most gorgeous yellow tulips she'd ever seen. Something flipped over inside her heart. Her family wasn't into sending flowers, and only one person here knew she loved yellow tulips.

There was a card with them. "Dinner tonight. Pine Lodge. All arranged. See you at seven."

Her throat swelled with emotion as she carried the vase over to a side table and set it down. They looked so stunning that she was about to race upstairs to get her camera, but then wondered if that was a good idea. Did she really want to take away more memories of Blake?

The telephone rang then.

It was Joel. Oh, Lord. She'd forgotten her date with him tonight. The tulips caught her eye and she knew she'd rather spend her last hours here in Aspen with Blake than go to the movies with Joel.

She opened her mouth to speak but before she could say anything, he apologized and told her that his cousin was in town overnight and this was his only chance to catch up with her. Did she mind? No. Could they go to the movies tomorrow night instead? She said she would let him know. She had no idea whether she would still be here tomorrow night. Then he mentioned that he was in town right now and would get the nurse to check on her later today, but she thanked him and said it wasn't necessary.

More than relieved, Samantha looked at the tulips as she hung up the telephone, Joel already relegated to the back of her mind. Blake might just want to discuss her job tonight, but right now she didn't care. She needed to know where it had all gone wrong this morning. More importantly, she wanted to know if there was even a slim chance it was something that could be fixed.

Seven

Samantha hadn't been sure what she should wear for tonight. While the flowers and the dinner were very thoughtful of Blake, and while he'd said he would give her an explanation as to why he walked away from her this morning in the bathroom and that sounded promising, none of that meant he *wanted* her.

In the end she decided to keep it fairly low-key, just like she would if she were dining with him for business reasons. She wore a thin brown sweater over cream slacks and a pair of low-heeled pumps, adding a gold chain at her neck to make it a little more stylish.

Just after six-thirty one of the hotel staff arrived as sunset spiked through the lodge. He placed a cooked casserole in the oven to keep warm, dessert in the refrigerator, then lit the log fire before beautifully setting the table in the small dining alcove. Had Blake requested the two candles on the table? She was about to ask the young waiter when Blake came in the front door.

"Blake!" she exclaimed, her pulse picking up at the sight of him. Realizing she might be giving herself away, she pulled herself back and toned it down. "You're early," she said more sedately. "I didn't expect you quite so soon."

"We had a tailwind." He nodded at the waiter. "It looks good, Andy. Thanks."

Samantha wasn't surprised that he knew the man's name. Blake was good with people—as long as you did the right thing by him.

"No problem, Mr. Jarrod." Andy's smile encompassed them both. "I'll come and collect everything tomorrow." He nodded good-night, then went through to the kitchen.

Blake stood there for a minute looking at Samantha, his eyes flicking down over her outfit then away. "I could do with a shower," he muttered, and made for the stairs.

She felt nervous all of a sudden. She twisted away herself. "I'll just make sure the food's okay." She left the room and went into the kitchen, glad that Andy was still gathering a couple of things together before he left. It brought the world back into focus and took it away from her and Blake. She needed the balance.

Andy left and she busied herself unnecessarily checking on the casserole, then poured herself a glass of water and stood there sipping it to calm her nerves. She could only stay in there so long, and soon she wandered back into the lounge area and drew the drapes against the encroaching night, before switching on the lamps.

It was too quiet, so she put on a CD to fill the silence

and sat down on the couch to wait. The wood scent from the burning logs in the fireplace wafted throughout the room, and after a few minutes, she could feel the soft music begin to ease the tension inside her. And then it hit her and she realized how romantic the whole place looked. She groaned slightly. It hadn't been intentional but would Blake believe that? It all looked so intimate.

Panicking that he might think she was trying to seduce him, she was about to about to jump up and turn off the music when she saw Blake coming down the stairs. He wasn't looking at her and she ate up the sight of him. He was so handsome in light gray pants and a navy crewneck sweater, but it was his magnetic aura of masculinity that caught her breath.

He reached the bottom step and all at once he glanced up and his gaze quickly summed up the ambiance in the room. She could feel warmth steal under her skin. This guy never missed a trick.

"You must be tired," she said, hoping to ignore what he might think was obvious.

"A little. It's been a long day."

And then their eyes met—memories of this morning between them.

She moistened her mouth. "Blake, I—"

He shook his head. "Not yet, Samantha. Let's eat first. I'm starving and I need to relax a little."

"Of course." She swung toward the kitchen. "I'll serve the dinner."

"I'll pour the wine."

She hurried away, expelling a shaky breath once she reached the privacy of the kitchen. Blake wouldn't discuss the matter until he was ready, so she would just have to have a little patience. Perhaps it would be best if she had some food in her stomach first.

When she came back carrying the plates of chicken casserole, he was sitting at the table, having poured the wine. He stood up as she approached and took the plates from her. He'd always been a gentleman where she was concerned, holding out her chair or opening doors for her. She knew it was something he did on autopilot.

"You lit the candles," she said for something to say. "They look really nice."

He put the plates down on the table. "Andy knows his job."

She wasn't sure if that meant Blake had asked for them or if Andy had merely improvised. Did it matter, she asked herself as he held her chair out just as she'd expected.

As she sat down, she glimpsed the tulips on the side table. That was probably why he'd looked at her strangely before going upstairs to change. He must think her so ungrateful.

"Oh, Blake, I should have said something earlier. Thank you so much for the tulips. They're absolutely gorgeous."

"You like them, then?" He looked pleased as he sat down opposite her.

"I love them."

He considered her. "You getting hit on the head was very good for me."

She blinked. "It was?"

"I learned two things about you. What your favorite flower is, and your favorite color."

"Want to know my favorite perfume, too?" she joked, touched by his words.

Only he didn't laugh. "It's Paris by Yves Saint Laurent," he said with an unexpected thickness to his voice that made her nerves tingle.

"You know?"

"You bought some the first time we went to Paris together, remember?" He made it sound like they'd been together in Paris for something other than business.

Surprised he remembered that time two years ago when she'd first gone to work for him, she dropped her gaze and fanned her napkin over her lap, though she rather felt like fanning her face instead. "This looks delicious."

There was a slight pause. "Yes."

She could feel his eyes on her as she picked up her fork and finally looked at him again. "So, what was the problem in Vegas that you needed to go there in such a hurry?"

A moment ticked by then he picked up his fork. "There was a problem with one of the chefs. He was being a bit too temperamental, and the kitchen staff was threatening to walk out. It was beginning to escalate into a big commotion with the unions. It started to get ugly."

"And it's sorted out now?"

"Of course."

She had to smile. "Naturally. You wouldn't have come back otherwise, right?"

Suddenly there was an air of watchfulness about him. "What happened to your date with Joel tonight?"

She'd wondered if he'd mention it. And then something else occurred to her. Could he have arranged to get Joel out of the way tonight? The thought made her pulse race. "His cousin's in Aspen for the night and he wanted to spend time with her." She tilted her head. "You didn't have anything to do with that, did you?"

His brow rose. "Me? Am I that good?"

"Yes!" she exclaimed on a half chuckle.

A flash of humor crossed his face. "Believe me, I'm not *that* clever."

It did sound silly now. Blake could make things happen, but this time he'd have to find Joel's cousin and get that person to come to Aspen. Why would he bother? He knew he merely had to send her flowers and arrange dinner and she'd capitulate like every woman before her.

"Anyway, how are you feeling?" he asked.

"Terrific."

He searched her face, then inclined his head as if satisfied. "At least you only worked half the day."

Her eyes widened. "How do you know that?"

"I checked with Erica. She said you'd left at lunch-time."

She smiled wryly. "Did she also tell you she checked on me nearly every hour after that?"

"She promised me she would."

Why was she *not* surprised? "That was a bit over the top, wasn't it?"

"I don't think so."

She tried not to look more into it than there was. He probably wanted her all better so he could get rid of her faster. Then she knew that wasn't fair of her and she pulled her thoughts back into line. "You always were concerned for your staff, Blake. Thank you."

He looked at her strangely, as if he couldn't under-stand why she was putting herself in with the rest of his staff. But if that were the case, didn't that mean he was thinking she was something more to him than she actually was?

God, she had to stop thinking so much!

She picked up her wineglass. "You know, Blake. Erica isn't as bad as you imagine her to be. I suspect she'd still have kept an eye on me even without you asking her." She took a sip of her drink but watched him carefully over the rim of her glass.

His brows furrowed. "I guess so." As much as he appeared to concede the point, he didn't look totally convinced about Erica's intentions.

Samantha understood why. "You think she's only doing something nice for a reason, don't you?"

"Maybe."

"Has it occurred to you that the reason is *you?*" She let him consider that, then added, "Maybe she wants to get to know her brother, and she knows the only way she can do that is to show him she is willing to help him out?"

"Maybe." He paused. "But she cares for you, too."

She felt a rush of affection for Erica. "And that goes to show she's a nice person and worthy of your friendship... if not your love."

His lips twisted. "The hit on the head seems to have muddled your brain. You think you're a psychoanalyst now, do you?"

"Where you're concerned I have to be," she said without thinking, but knew it was her mention of the word *love* that had got his back up. Love and Blake Jarrod did *not* go hand-in-hand.

And neither did Samantha Thompson.

Not with love.

Certainly not with Blake Jarrod.

A curious look passed over his face. "Why would you want to psychoanalyze me anyway?"

This time she thought before speaking. No use giving away more of herself than she needed to. It was best she keep up a wall. He would appreciate her more for that.

She managed a thin smile. "A person likes to figure out how their boss's mind works. It helps with the job."

He leaned back in his chair. "Yes, you were always good at that."

Then…just as she thought she had it all under control, all at once everything rose in her throat. She couldn't take any more of this subterfuge and talking around things that mattered. "Blake, don't you think it's time we talked about last night? You took such good care of me, and then this morning…"

He stilled. "Yes?"

She swallowed hard. She had to ask the next question and she had to be prepared to accept the answer. "I'd like to know what I did wrong."

His face blanched as he sat forward. "Nothing, Samantha. You did nothing wrong."

"Then what—"

He drew a breath. "Samantha, are you a virgin?"

She felt her cheeks heat up. "No."

He looked surprised. "I thought you might be."

"Well, I'm not," she said, hunching her shoulders, wondering where this was going to lead.

His expression softened a little. "But you're not very experienced, are you?"

Okay, so it led to further embarrassment.

She could feel her cheeks redden further. "You must know I…er…haven't been with a lot of men."

"How many?"

Her eyes widened. "None of your business."

"You made it my business this morning."

She hesitated, then, "One lover when I was a teenager."

His brow rose. "And none since?" He must have read her thoughts. "You can tell me. I'm not going to tell anyone else."

So, okay, she would accept that. "Well, there was a man back home…."

He didn't blink an eye but she knew she had his attention. "And?"

"We didn't become lovers, but I was in love with him."

"What happened?"

Her lips twisted with self-derision. "He wasn't in love with me."

Blake nodded. "That explains why you haven't had any relationships since I've known you," he said, almost to himself. Then his eyes sharpened. "Are you still in love with him?"

"No. Carl left to go overseas and ended up marrying someone else. I realized I'd been in love with the *idea* of love and that's all it was." She sighed. "But it was a good lesson in learning that you can never be sure of another person's feelings." Realizing that she was suddenly giving too much away, she tried to be casual. "So, you see, I can only lay claim to one lover and that was a long time ago."

"I could tell."

Her composure lurched like a drunken sailor. "I'm sorry. I thought my enthusiasm might make up for any lack of experience."

"Don't apologize. Your enthusiasm was great. Damn great," he said brusquely. "I had a hard time walking away from you."

Her heart faltered. "You did? I thought you didn't want me."

He expelled a harsh breath. "Did my body *feel* like I didn't want you?"

She remembered the tense cords of his body burning her flesh through her nightshirt. "No," she croaked, then had to clear her throat before speaking again. "But what do I know anyway? I thought a man could easily turn it off and on." Carl certainly had been able to put a stop to anything beyond a few kisses.

"I'm not made of stone like that other guy," Blake scoffed, reading her mind, but his voice had gentled. "And all this goes to prove to me that I did the right thing this morning. I'm the experienced one here and that means I have a responsibility to you. I'm glad now I didn't take something from you that you might regret giving later on."

"You mean my virginity?" Her heart rose in her chest at the respect he'd afforded her.

"Yes."

"But I'm *not* a virgin," she pointed out.

"I know that now."

He'd rejected her all for nothing? It was admirable, but… "You should have asked me at the time."

He pursed his mouth. "It's not only that," he said, sending her stomach plummeting.

"I see."

"No, I don't think you do." He clenched his jaw. "You were so damn generous, Samantha. You were giving me everything and I was worried that you…er…might look more into this than you should. I just wasn't sure you could handle any emotional involvement."

She appreciated where he was coming from with this, but her heart still managed to drop at his words. What *was* it about her that every man felt they had to warn her off?

"Don't worry," she assured him. "I'm not planning on repeating history and losing my heart to anyone in the future."

His eyes searched hers. "Are you sure?"

"Positive." Suddenly she felt all-knowing. "Maybe it's *you* who can't handle it, Blake."

He looked startled, then scowled. "I admit it. I can't. And to be blunt, I don't want to even try." He paused. "But this isn't about me. I'm thinking of *you,* Samantha. Not me."

Her heart tilted. She appreciated his honesty but she could look after herself. And to be equally as honest, how could she give him up without a fight now that she knew he wanted her?

"Blake, thank you for that but you're doing me an injustice. I'm a grown woman. I know sex doesn't always mean commitment. I have needs and I know my own mind. I know what I want, and while I'm here…" She looked him straight in the eye. "What I want is *you.*"

"Hell."

She flinched. "I'm sorry if that makes things more difficult."

"Don't be. It's your directness, that's all. It blows me away."

She felt a rush of warmth. "I do want you, Blake. Very much."

"Your head—"

"Is on the mend." She paused, preempting him. "And yes, I'm sure."

His eyes flared sensuously. "Then do me a favor."

She moistened her mouth. "What?"

"Go upstairs and put your nightshirt on for me," he said, his voice turning heavy with huskiness.

She blinked in surprise. "My nightshirt?"

"You looked so sexy in it this morning. I've been thinking about it all day. It's been driving me crazy."

Sudden awareness danced in her veins. "Does this mean we're going to—"

"Have sex? Yes." A tiny pulse beat in his cheekbone. "But only if you're sure you can handle a purely sexual relationship," he said, giving her one last out.

Excitement washed over her. He still wanted her.

She nodded. "I can handle it, Blake."

"Then go change."

She got to her feet. It was now or never. And right now *never* definitely wasn't an option.

Samantha couldn't deny she was nervous as she came out of her room in her nightshirt and descended the staircase in a pair of high-heeled gold sandals she'd put on at the last moment. The bottom button was missing from her nightshirt, but the material covered her and what did it matter now anyway?

Blake had turned the lamps off and stood by the log fire, watching her in the flickering light with the same look he'd had on his face last Saturday night when she'd dressed for her date with Joel. She'd been trying to capture Blake's attention that night to make him jealous. Tonight she'd definitely caught more than his attention.

Tonight they both knew they would be a part of each other. The power of that thought stunned her.

"Come over here, Samantha," he said huskily when she reached the bottom step. The air throbbed between them and she quivered, moving forward without a falter as she made her away across the carpet to him.

His blue eyes moved slowly down over her, and something flared in them. "You're still missing the button," he said, as if to himself.

She blinked in surprise as she reached him. "You knew it was missing?"

"Oh, yes. It came off this morning in the bathroom... when I lifted you up on the sink."

She could feel herself go hot all over. "Oh. I hadn't realized."

"I know you didn't," he said, with a pointed look. He pulled her up against him. "God, you're so damn sexy, Samantha Thompson," he murmured, gathering her close. "My very sexy lady." His body was hard and she trembled. "Now, does that feel like I can turn myself off so easily?" he said thickly, his breath stirring over her face.

The solid warmth of him pressed against her stomach. "No." The word emerged on a whisper.

"There's no going back this time," he said, reassuring that this time he would not walk away.

The deepest longing stirred within her. "Kiss me, Blake."

He did.

Once...twice...long and slow...

And then he eased back and looked deep into her eyes.

She looked back at him.

Blue on blue.

"I want you in front of the fire," he murmured, sending her pulse jumping all over the place. "Here. Lie down on the cushions." She saw he had placed two big cushions near their feet. "Be careful of your head," he said, helping to lower her to the thick rug, so sweet and caring. She wanted to say it was too late, that she was about to lose her head anyway, only the words wouldn't come.

Soon she was lying there in her nightshirt and her gold sandals and he was standing over her in the firelight, his gaze scanning the full length of her, before stopping at the junction to her thighs. "You left your panties on," he mused throatily, telling her the front of her nightshirt must have fallen open at the hem.

She moistened her mouth. "I wanted to take them off, but..."

"I'll be happy to do the honors..." he said, and her heartbeat quickened, "but in a minute."

All at once she wanted him so much. "Take off your clothes first, Blake. Don't make me wait."

His eyes darkened and he dragged his sweater up over his head, along with his T-shirt, tossing them aside. He kicked off his shoes and his hands went to his belt....

He hesitated.

"Your trousers, too." She was desperate to see him fully as a man for the first time, the thought making her lightheaded.

Another second, then his hands dropped away from the buckle. "Not yet." He dropped to his knees beside her, and let his gaze slide along the full length of her, like he was committing her to memory.

But his bare chest beckoned her and she reached

out to touch him, her fingers tingling as she came into contact with the dark whorls of hair over hard muscle. He groaned and slammed his hand over hers, stopping it from moving.

"Not yet," he repeated, putting her hand back down beside her.

And then with slow deliberation he began to undo her top button. She gasped as he undid another and slid her nightshirt off her shoulder a little. "I've wanted to do this since this morning," he murmured, lowering his head and trailing a kiss from the curve of her shoulder to her throat, then down to the valley between her breasts.

He inhaled deeply, then lifted his face and undid another button, exposing her breasts. Soon he was leaning over her, using his mouth to possess the tip of one nipple before moving to the other, gliding his tongue back and forth over them, imprinting them with his taste.

"Oh, my God," she muttered, shuddering at such an exquisite touch. "I…"

"Steady, my lovely." He shifted back a little. Another button undone allowed him to drift kisses along the exposed skin to her belly button. She shuddered again when he stroked his palm over her stomach, before the rest of the buttons were unfastened and the material finally parted, falling away to her sides and revealing her near-nakedness to him.

"Beautiful," he murmured, dipping his fingers under the waistband then peeling the panties down her body. By the time he'd finished, he'd moved to kneel between her thighs. She moaned faintly, suspecting a blush was rolling all the way down to her feet.

"So beautiful." He slowly reached out and slipped a

finger through the triangle of curls, making her gasp. "You like that?"

She moaned again. "Oh, yes."

For long, heart-stopping moments he toyed with her dampening skin, sending tremors through her. And then he slid his hands under her, cupping the cheeks of her bottom and tilting her lower body up to him, the satin material of her nightshirt falling away fully as his head lowered to the dark V at her thighs.

But before he touched, he stopped and looked up again, his eyes catching hers, holding still. He didn't speak or move a muscle, but there was a primitive look in his eyes that swept her breath away.

Slowly he lowered his head again and sought her out, his mouth beginning a slow worship of her femininity. She gasped as his tongue slid between her folds, teasing and tantalizing her, stroking her in erotic exploration, taking her to the brink, then bringing her back…once… twice…then finally he took her right over the edge, any remnants of her control disintegrating as she pulsed with the purest of pleasures.

Long moments later, she was still trying to recover when he rose to his feet and stripped off his trousers. She watched mesmerized as he put on a condom, thrilled that she had the power to make this man so hot and hard for her.

He was soon kneeling back down between her legs, and kissing his way right up the center of her until he found her mouth. He gave her one long kiss, then suddenly he was part of her.

In her.

She held him deep inside, finally one with Blake

Jarrod. She'd been waiting so long. It was the most wonderful feeling in the world.

He kissed her deeper as he began to thrust, long strokes time after time. Soon she began to tremble around him, toppling over the edge again, the flickering of the flames in the fireplace nothing compared to their own fire burning within.

Samantha lay amongst the cushions in front of the fire and watched Blake stride toward the downstairs bathroom. He'd covered her with the throw from the couch, and she enjoyed lying there watching his bare back and buttocks that were all firm muscle and arrestingly male.

She smiled to herself in the gentle glow from the fireplace. She couldn't believe it. She'd made love with Blake. She felt marvelous. He'd been so generous and loving and…

All at once, she found herself blinking back sudden tears. Their lovemaking had been so much more than sex. She hadn't admitted it to herself until now lest she back out, but when he'd said earlier they were having sex, something had gnawed at her as she'd gone up the stairs. It had sounded like they would merely be having sex for sex's sake. And while that was somewhat true, that wasn't what she was *only* about.

She'd known the same was true for Blake. He'd already proven that by not taking advantage this morning when he'd thought she was a virgin. She'd "made love" with Blake, despite love not being involved. There was respect between them and that was more important to her.

Right then she heard him coming back and she

quickly blinked away any suggestion of tears. He wouldn't want to know. Otherwise he'd think she *hadn't* been able to handle it, when it was merely because she hadn't expected to be quite so touched by all this.

He gave a sexy smile as he dropped down and leaned over to kiss her. "How do you feel?" he murmured, pulling back and looking into her eyes.

She was fully aware of his nakedness next to her. She could easily reach out and touch him. "Wonderful."

He looked pleased as he lifted the throw and slid under it to lie on his back, pulling her against his chest and kissing the top of her head but being careful of her injury. "Is that better?"

She was glad he couldn't look into her eyes. "Much."

He chuckled, his breath stirring her hair. "Who knew, eh?"

"What?"

"That we'd be so good together."

She'd never doubted it. "We work well together in business, so why not in bed?"

"True."

After that, they lay in quiet. The fire crackled and the clock on the wall ticked the seconds by. Samantha began to feel sleepy. There was no place she'd rather be in the world right now, she thought, as her eyelids drifted shut and she listened to the tick tock…tick tock…tick…*she loved him*…tock.

Startled, she jumped. Dear God, *she loved him.*

"What's wrong?"

Her brain stumbled. Panic whorled inside her. The ability to speak deserted her for a moment…and then somehow she pulled herself together. "What? Oh, nothing. I think I fell asleep too fast."

"Don't worry. There's no chance of that happening again just yet." He put his hand under her chin, lowering his head and lifting her mouth up to his. She quickly closed her eyes, hiding them from him, hiding her deepest secret. She'd betrayed him by falling in love with him. And she'd betrayed herself. She hadn't wanted to love him. She had never intended for that to happen.

Then he kissed her and the slow, delicious process of making love to her started again. She prayed to God for the strength not to reveal her love for this man who was leaving his mark on her like no one had ever done before. She couldn't afford to give her feelings away, or their relationship would be over before it had really begun. Wanting Blake had been hard enough.

Loving him was going to be intolerable.

<u>Eight</u>

Blake made love to her many times during the night, both downstairs and in his bed. Samantha had never known such bliss, but by the time the next morning rolled around and she'd gone back to her own room to get dressed for work, she had a thousand worries inside her head. She loved Blake and that presented so many problems. She'd virtually promised him she wouldn't fall for him. Now it seemed like she'd gone back on her word.

Worse, somewhere along the line she hadn't exactly "fallen" for him. No, she'd skipped that bit and had progressed straight to loving him. They'd worked together so closely these past two years, she already knew Blake was the type of man she admired and respected. And falling "in" love implied she could fall "out" of love with him—like she'd done with Carl. With

Blake, she knew there would be no retracting her love for him.

If only she could.

Oh, God, loving Blake had taken her further with her emotions than she'd ever dared venture. And now she had to survive until she could leave for good. She had to remain tough. She would constantly have to keep something of herself back. Last night during their lovemaking, she'd only managed to keep a lid on it through sheer terror—only by telling herself he would run in the other direction if he knew how deep her feelings went. Talk about emotional involvement on her part!

And now more than ever she had to leave at the end of her month's contract. She couldn't stay permanently. Blake had been honest enough to admit he couldn't handle emotional involvement and she believed him. If he discovered she loved him, he'd be horrified. He'd probably have her on the next plane out of Aspen before she could blink. Even if he didn't, she couldn't risk giving him such a strong emotive power over her. A power he might use in and out of the bedroom to get her to stay.

For all the wrong reasons.

Yet would Blake manipulate her in such a way? He was, after all, the man she loved. An honorable man. Would he really do any of those things? Her heart remembered his generous lovemaking and said no. Her head remembered the hard businessman and said maybe.

Making love to a woman certainly changed things, Blake decided as he watched Samantha eat breakfast in the hotel restaurant. He'd sat opposite her like this many times in the last two years but it had always been about work. Now all he could think about was being inside her again.

She'd been so generously tight last night when he'd finally buried himself in her softness. It had almost sent him straight into orgasm. Only the need to give her more pleasure had held him back. Never before had that happened to him. He'd always made sure his partner had been fulfilled before taking his own pleasure, but this time her pleasure had been totally his. It had been the ultimate experience for him. How could that other man—that Carl—not have wanted her in his bed? Idiot!

"Tell me something, Blake," she said, cutting into his thoughts as he buttered a slice of toast.

"Anything." Well, not quite anything. He wasn't up for a meaningful discussion this morning. He merely wanted to sit here and soak up this beautiful woman in front of him.

She tilted her brunette head to one side. "Did you tell Andy to add the candles last night at dinner?"

He was relieved at the simple question. "Sorry, no. I wasn't planning on seduction. At least, not until I was sure you could handle becoming my lover." He smiled. "I'll light you some candles tonight, though."

A feathery blush ran across her cheeks but she looked pleased. "I've just realized something. You're a romantic, Blake Jarrod."

"Sometimes." He liked to romance a woman as much as the next guy. "But don't get the wrong idea that I'm a softie."

She nodded. "Got it. Hard in business. Good in bed."

He gave a low laugh. "I like that assessment." He also liked to think he was both things in and out of bed, but he wouldn't embarrass her further. Not here.

But tonight…

"I keep forgetting to mention this," she said, "but I haven't thanked you for taking such good care of me the other night."

"Oh, I think you did thank me," he said pointedly. "And you can thank me again later."

"Blake!" she hissed, but he could see she was enjoying this sexual interplay.

"What?" he drawled. "I'm just saying—"

A figure appeared at their table. "There you are, Sam," Joel said, giving them both a smile but causing Blake's mouth to clamp shut. "I'm glad I caught you. How are you this morning? How's the head?"

"Fine, Joel. No aftereffects at all," she assured the doctor.

"You're taking things easy, I hope?"

Her eyes made a quick dart across the table then back up at the other man. "Yes." Her cheeks had grown a little warm and that in itself appeased Blake.

"Good. Then how about we take in that movie tonight?"

She looked at Blake again. "Oh, Joel, I'm sorry, I can't."

"Tomorrow night, then?"

Blake held his tongue. He wanted to lay claim to Samantha and tell the other man to shove off, but he'd first give her the opportunity to do it.

"Um, Joel. Perhaps not." She shifted in her seat. "I'm returning to Vegas in less than two weeks' time and then I'm going home to Pasadena for good once I wrap things up there. So, you see, there's a lot to be done here right now. I need to work full-on with Blake until then."

Blake was dumbfounded.

"You're leaving?" the other man said, sounding shocked, echoing Blake's thoughts. "I can't believe that."

Another echo of his thoughts.

She looked slightly uncomfortable. "Yes, I know. I'm sorry I didn't tell you, but it was something that hadn't been finalized until now."

Joel gave a small nod. "I understand. Maybe we can get together in Pasadena sometime in the future? We'll at least have to get together for coffee before you leave."

She slipped him a smile. "That would be lovely."

Blake was vaguely aware of the other man walking away from the table, but he only had eyes for one person. "Samantha," he growled. "What the hell is going on?"

Her look seemed cagey. "I didn't want him knowing the truth. Our affair is our business and no one else's."

Anger stirred inside him. "I'm not talking about our affair, and you know it. Dammit, don't tell me you don't know what I'm talking about."

She lifted her chin. "You're talking about me still leaving," she clarified. "I'm sorry, Blake. Did you think that I would change my mind?"

"Yes, I damn well did." He'd expected her to stay now, not because he'd enticed her into staying but because she *wanted* to. And hell, she didn't seem to understand that he'd made a big concession in not seducing her in the bathroom yesterday morning. Now it felt like she'd slapped him in the face. He'd given. She'd taken. And now she was giving nothing back.

"But why, Blake? Our lovemaking hasn't changed

anything. We both decided it would only be physical and nothing more. No commitment, remember?"

Her words appeared to be reasonable, but for all that she had a peculiar look in her eyes he couldn't decipher. "That's still got nothing to do with you leaving."

"Doesn't it? I was leaving before we made love and I'm still leaving, so what's changed?"

Damn her. She was right. Even so, he couldn't explain it. He just knew something *had* changed and he didn't want to decode it. He just wanted her to stay and enjoy what they had for a while. They could at least get a couple of months together. Why leave while the going was good?

She shot him an unexpected candid look. "Blake, you asked me if I could handle a sexual relationship, and I said I could. It sounds to me like *you* aren't handling it."

His mouth tightened. "I'm handling it."

She shook her head. "No, I don't—"

"Blake," a male voice called out, and Blake instantly knew who it was. He stiffened. Damn the world! His twin brother was the last person he wanted to see. Guy had always understood him—sometimes more than he understood himself. Right now wasn't a good time to put that to the test.

He shot to his feet, turned and headed for the private elevator. "It'll have to wait until later, Guy," he muttered, striding past his brother.

Guy's steps faltered as he approached the table. Then as he came closer, he looked at Samantha with mild amusement. "Was it something I said?" he quipped in that easygoing way of his.

Samantha couldn't smile if her life depended on it. "He's got a lot on his mind."

Guy sobered. "Yeah, I know." He sent her a penetrating look that reminded her of Blake. "I hear you're leaving."

She nodded, still surprised word had gotten around the family so fast, and even more surprised that they were genuinely sorry to see her go. It wasn't like she was a friend of the family...or marrying into it.

"I'm glad I saw you," Guy said, drawing her back to the moment. "Avery and I would like to have you around for dinner before you go."

Somehow she managed a faint smile. "That would be very nice."

"Blake, too, of course." Silence, then, "He'll miss you when you leave."

"Maybe." *Maybe not.* "I'll find him an excellent replacement."

"It won't be the same."

Her throat constricted. "He'll get over it." She stood up. "You'll have to excuse me, Guy. I need to start work. There's a lot to do."

Guy stepped back and let her pass, but he was frowning and she could feel his eyes on her all the way out the eatery. Thankfully she had a few moments of privacy as the elevator took her to the top floor.

If only Blake wanted her to stay because he loved her, then things would be perfect. But for him this was only about two things—the job and sex. It wasn't about love. She sighed. She'd have to be crazy to think he would make a commitment. And she hadn't wanted a commitment before anyway, so why the heck was she even considering it now?

She must have rocks in her head.

Or have been hit *on* the head with a rock. It must have caused more damage than she'd thought. Why else would she be unwise enough to love a man who wouldn't let himself love in return? That bruise must have addled more than her brain. It had addled her heart.

Thankfully Blake's door was shut when she entered her office so she sat at her desk. Come to think of it, she felt a little better knowing she had hoisted Blake with his own petard. That was rather clever of her. He'd sprouted all that talk about not getting emotionally involved, but clearly his emotions *were* involved, albeit not enough and not the ones that mattered most to her.

They didn't entail love.

God was merciful just then, when not only did the phone start to ring but one of the staff who had a meeting with Blake walked into her office. Samantha got busy, putting on her professional persona as she placed the caller on hold, buzzing Blake on the intercom to tell him his first appointment was here. At his request, she ushered the staff member into his office, all the while keeping her face neutral whenever she looked at her boss. He seemed equally as disinterested in her, though she knew otherwise. What he was and what he seemed were two different things. She could recognize that in another person. After all, wasn't she an expert at the same thing?

Midmorning while Blake was busy at a staff meeting in the Great Room, Samantha picked up the telephone with a heavy heart and did what she had to do. She called Mary Wentworth back and spoke to her about a replacement. The other woman was surprised to hear she was leaving, but was more than happy to help. Mary promised she would e-mail some résumés of suitable applicants within a few hours.

Blake returned after the meeting, formally asked if there were any messages, then strode straight into his office. Samantha's heart sank at how cold he was, but there was nothing she could do about it. She still had to leave.

At lunchtime she had some sandwiches sent up from the kitchen, and Blake made it apparent that he preferred to eat at his desk by himself, with his door closed between them. Usually they ate together while discussing work. Or if they ate at their own desks, the door remained open.

Not this time.

And that was fine with her, she decided, growing more and more upset. She needed a filter to stop the waves of anger coming out of his office anyway. To clear her head, she went for a walk in the fresh air. Blake didn't ask where she'd been when she returned and she didn't offer. It was plain to see he was no longer concerned about her.

By late afternoon, Samantha had had enough of his attitude. He'd chastised her after she'd put through a call he hadn't wanted to take. He'd found fault with a letter she'd typed up for his signature. And he'd told her to go recheck some figures on a report that she knew were correct.

When she brought the report back, she deliberately placed another folder on top of it.

His head shot up. "What's this?"

"Résumés. They all come highly recommended."

His lips flattened. "I didn't ask you to do this."

She angled her chin. "It's what you pay me to do."

"I pay you to do what you're told."

She gasped, then held herself rigid. "That's unfair of you. You don't mind me being proactive in other things with my job. It's why I'm such a good assistant and you know it."

"We're talking fairness now, are we? *You're* the one leaving *me*. How fair is that?"

"I'm not leaving *you,* Blake," she lied. "Anyway, don't take it personally, remember? That's what you said to me when you reminded me of my contract obligations."

He muttered a curse, but for Samantha the last straw had already broken the camel's back. "I can't continue under these conditions, Blake. If you won't treat me right, then I'll pack my things and leave tonight. And I don't care if you take me to court for breach of contract either." She hesitated, but only for a second. "I believe I could make a good case for justifying my leaving anyway, considering the personal turn our relationship has taken."

There was a lengthy silence.

His eyes challenged hers. "Would you go that far?"

She gave a jerky nod. "If pushed I would. Don't doubt that."

He held her gaze with narrowed eyes.

And then suddenly something happened and a suspicion of admiration began to glint in them. "Way to go!" he said softly, startling her. "You're a tough little madam. I always knew you could hold your own in your job, but I never thought to see the day when you used it against *me*."

A little of the tension went out of her. "So things will return to normal?" she asked cautiously.

"No."

Her heart dropped.

"Things can never be normal between us again. Not since last night." He drew a long breath, as if taking a moment before making a decision. "I don't want to see you go, but I don't want to keep you here against your will either. If you want to go then I have to accept it."

It wasn't what she wanted at all.

It was what she *had* to do.

"Thank you, Blake."

"But at least stay until your contract runs out." He waited a moment. "I'm not asking for the job and I'm not asking for the sex. I'm asking for *me*."

She caught her breath. This was the best she could hope for, the best it could get, and she wasn't about to argue with that. She would take her happiness where she could.

A whisper of joy filled her. "Okay, yes. I'll stay until my contract runs out, Blake," she said, and watched him let out a shuddering breath that touched her greatly. He really *did* want her to stay so that he could be with her.

Clearly satisfied now they were back on an even keel, he leaned back in his chair with a look she had no trouble translating. "Go over there and lock the door."

A tiny shiver of anticipation went down her spine. "Blake, I can't… I don't…"

"You can." His eyes turned deeper blue. "I seriously need to make love to you, Samantha."

Her heart tilted. Oh, she wanted that, too. She darted a look at the door. "The others—"

"Will think we don't want to be disturbed." He gave a crooked smile. "And they'd be right." He waited a moment. "You can always race into my washroom if anyone comes."

Wanting this…wanting him…she went and locked the heavy wood door, but ducked her head out into her office first to make sure no one was there. "I can't believe I'm doing this," she muttered, turning the lock.

"Don't think about it." He looked amused and she decided that if he wanted her, then he was going to have her. And she would wipe that amusement right off his face.

Fingers going to the buttons of her long-sleeved blouse, she began to undo each one as she approached him across the plush carpet.

One eyebrow lifted. "Are you teasing me, Miss Thompson?"

"Actually I think I am."

He smiled, and she smiled, then his smile started to slip as she completely undid the blouse, leaving it hanging open over her black bra. She marveled at where this seductress in her was coming from, but didn't let it deter her. She wasn't about to waste a minute of it.

She reached the side of the desk. "More?"

"Oh, yeah."

"You're the boss."

Her hands were shaking a little as she slid the zipper of her slacks down, pushing them and her panties all the way to the floor, then stepped out of them. She heard a rasping sound escape Blake's throat and there was a blaze in his eyes that seemed to emit from his whole body.

Gratified by his reaction…satisfied by his amusement now turned to desire…she climbed onto his lap, knees on either side of his thighs, her blouse covering her bra—and then only just.

After that, passion overtook all rational thoughts and the air hummed with soft, sensual sounds.

Nine

They dined together back at Pine Lodge, then made love again that night, and when Samantha woke the next morning she lay there and wallowed in a sense of occasion. Her memories of them together like this were all she could take away with her. Her heart, she would leave with Blake.

He woke up then and made slow love to her again. Afterward she put on a bright face and they went about their business as usual, neither of them showing any outward sign to the others that they were lovers. They hadn't discussed it, but Samantha was glad about it. Already his family seemed to have taken a special interest in them, and she didn't want anyone guessing she loved him.

Late morning, Samantha left her office and went down to the hotel kitchen to get some fresh milk for their coffee. She could have phoned down for it but she needed to stretch her legs.

In the hallway, she ran into Erica. They chatted a few moments but Samantha could see the other woman was preoccupied. "Erica, is something wrong?"

Erica wrinkled her nose. "Yes, unfortunately. I've been arranging a surprise party for tonight for this man who lives in town. It's for his wife's fortieth birthday and she thinks she's coming here for dinner." She clicked her tongue. "I've been working on this for weeks."

"So what's the problem?"

"We've got a DJ for later in the evening, but the husband particularly asked for someone to play piano music in the background during the meal, and now the piano player has come down sick." Her smooth forehead creased as she began thinking out loud. "The DJ could probably play some soft music as an alternative, but I really don't want to disappoint the husband. He said his wife loves the piano and he wants to give her the best party. I was hoping there might be someone in town I could find, but it's probably too late."

All the while she was talking, Samantha's heart began thumping with a mixture of excitement and panic. "You may not believe this," she said, not believing she was actually saying this, "but I can help."

Erica's eyes brightened. "You can? Do you know someone who plays the piano?"

"Yes." *Did she really want to say this?* "Me."

Erica stopped and blinked. "*You* play the piano?" She grimaced. "Sorry, that came out wrong. I just mean—"

Samantha smiled a little. "I know what you meant."

Regardless, Erica still looked doubtful. "You *really* play the piano?"

Samantha nodded. "Yes, *really*."

"You're sure?"

Samantha chuckled as her anxiety faded. "Lead the way to the piano and I'll show you. Just don't expect perfection. I have to tell you I'm a bit rusty."

Erica began to grin. "As long as it's not 'Chopsticks,' then I'll be happy. Follow me."

A few minutes later, Samantha did a warm-up then started playing a quick medley of popular tunes. Her fingers felt a bit stiff because she hadn't played since last Christmas at home in Pasadena, but she was soon enjoying herself—and enjoying the look on Erica's face.

"That's wonderful!" Erica murmured, once the music ended.

Samantha smiled with relief that she hadn't lost her touch nor made a fool of herself. "Thanks, but it's nothing special."

Erica shook her head. "No, you're very good."

"Not really."

"Yes, *really*," Erica teased. "Good Lord, I didn't know we had Liberace living here at the resort."

Samantha laughed. "Just be grateful my mother made me take piano lessons growing up."

"Oh, I am. Play some more, Samantha." All at once Erica's eyes widened and she chuckled. "Oh, my God, I don't believe I'm about to say this but 'play it again, Sam.'"

Samantha laughed. She knew she needed the practice so she was happy to oblige and felt more confident with each touch of the keys.

Afterward, they talked for five minutes then Samantha continued on her way to get the milk. Blake had a business lunch in town and had already left by the time she returned to the office, so she didn't get to tell him about it all until late afternoon.

He fell back in his chair. "*You* play the piano?"

A wry smile tugged at her mouth. "Why is that so far-fetched?"

"I don't know." Then he shook his head as if he wasn't hearing right. "Let me get this straight. *You're* going to play the piano at a party here at the resort tonight?"

She shrugged. "It's just background music during dinner." But she wasn't quite so calm inside, and talking about it now was making her kind of nervous.

He tilted his head at her. "Why didn't you tell me you could play the piano?"

"It wasn't a job requirement," she joked, more to calm her growing anxiety than anything.

His mouth quirked. "No, I guess it wasn't."

Her humor over, she bit her lip. "Actually, do you mind if I leave a little early? I need to get myself ready and I'd like some time to myself."

He gave a wayward smile. "You creative types are all alike."

"Blake—"

"Feel free to leave early," he agreed. Then his eyes slowly settled on her mouth. "But before you go…" Hunger jumped the distance between them. "I do think there is one requirement of your job that needs revisiting."

She knew what he was getting at. Her heart raced with a growing excitement. "Blake, we can't make love in here every afternoon."

"Who said we can't?"

"But I have to go now," she said, knowing she was weakening.

"In a minute," he murmured, sending her an intimate look across the desk. "Come and give me a kiss goodbye first."

She wagged a finger at him. "That's all, Blake. One kiss and no more."

"Trust me."

She moved toward him. "Okay…"

Half an hour later she left the office a very satisfied woman, amused at how easily she had fallen for his trickery. Of course, she couldn't fully blame her boss. She'd *wanted* to fall for it.

"Lady, you're far too dangerous to let loose on our male guests," Blake said, watching Samantha step into high heels. She wore a beaded jacket over black evening pants that flattered her slim figure, and she'd curled the brunette strands of her hair into a bubbly halo around her gorgeous face.

"You think I look okay?"

"More than okay. You'll knock 'em dead." He stepped closer and went to pull her toward him but she put a hand against his chest, stopping him.

"Wait! You'll mess up my lipstick."

Blake was amused. "I'd like to mess up more than your lipstick, beautiful."

Her blue eyes smiled back at him. "You already did that this afternoon. 'Trust me,' remember?"

He gave a low chuckle. "I remember." Even now he felt the stirrings of desire, so he stepped away from temptation. "Come on. I'll drive you up to the Manor."

"I can call the valet."

"That's okay. I want to look over those documents Gavin gave me about the new bungalow. It'll be a good chance to study them without the phones ringing." It was an excuse but she looked so good that he wanted to make sure she got home okay. If anyone hit on her they'd be sorry.

Ten minutes later they walked down the corridor toward the ballroom, but as they got closer she suddenly stopped. "Blake, please. Don't come in with me. You'll only make me more nervous."

"Okay. I'll be in the office until you're ready to go home."

"But—"

He leaned forward and dropped a kiss on her forehead. "I'll wait for you."

He looked up and saw Erica and Christian coming toward them. They were a distance away so he nodded at them then turned and walked in the other direction, taking the private elevator up to the office. He didn't care that they'd seen the kiss. He *did* care that they might think Samantha was his weak spot.

Christian had proven his integrity months ago, but the other man had his own weak point—Erica. It could make him blind to whatever his fiancée was up to, Blake thought, then winced. She may not be up to anything at all, he corrected, aware his hard attitude toward his half sister was diminishing with each passing day.

Yet he couldn't discount Erica was fooling him as well as Christian, though he was feeling less and less that was the case. He was usually a pretty good judge of character—when emotions weren't involved. Unfortunately finding out he had a half sister *had* brought out an emotional response in him. He hadn't liked that.

And he didn't like the emotional response he was feeling now as he sat down at his desk and saw the file with the résumés. It all came back that Samantha was actually going to leave. It had either been let her go in three weeks' time or lose her now. He hadn't been able to bear the thought of the latter.

And he wasn't up to reading those résumés right now either, he decided, putting them to the side. He would deal with it when he had to and not before.

He wasn't sure how long he'd been working when he heard piano music drift up from the bottom floor. He sat back in his chair and listened. Samantha was clearly talented as she went from one tune to another, even throwing in some classical music. He heard clapping at the end of that one, though whether it was for Samantha or in honor of the birthday guest, he wasn't sure. The music started up in another medley of popular tunes, so he figured it was for Samantha.

And rightly so.

Unable to stop himself, he knew he had to see her play in person and not merely listen from afar. He got up from his desk and went downstairs, hearing the clink of glasses and cutlery and the murmur of voices, but it was the music that drew him as he approached the ballroom.

Pushing open one of the large doors, he slipped inside and stood at the back, watching people half listening and half talking as Samantha played another piece of classical music. She didn't see him, but she appeared totally at ease at the piano, concentrating on the music, her hands flowing across the keys, looking very feminine and beautiful. Suddenly he was so proud of her that a lump rose in his throat.

"She's good," a female voice murmured, and he glanced sideways at an attractive woman in her late thirties who'd come to stand beside him.

He wasn't interested. "Yes," he said, looking back at Samantha.

"You're new here." She thrust a manicured hand in front of him. "I'm Clarice, by the way."

It would have been rude not to shake her hand, but he still wasn't interested. "Blake." He wished the woman would leave him alone so that he could concentrate on Samantha.

"Do you know the guest of honor?"

For a moment he thought she meant Samantha, then he realized she was talking about the birthday lady. "A casual acquaintance." He didn't feel the need to explain.

"I went to boarding school with Anne. We've been lifelong friends."

"That's great." The music ended on a high note and everyone started to clap and it gave him the chance to move away. "Excuse me," he said, taking a step.

Clarice put her hand on his arm, stopping him. "Would you care to have a drink later?"

He'd been approached like this many times but for some reason now he found it distasteful, though he hid it. He only wanted to see Samantha. "I'm sorry," he said, being as nice as possible so as not to offend. "Not tonight." He walked away.

And headed straight for Samantha getting up from the piano. She was laughing as some people rushed to talk to her, and as Blake weaved his way through the tables he could only think how much she lit up the room.

Then she saw him. "Blake," she murmured, her blue eyes lighting up *for him,* sending an extraordinary feeling soaring inside his chest.

He reached her and put his hand on her elbow. "I think the lady needs a drink," he told the group at large, making no apologies as he led her away.

"What are you doing here?" she said as he took her over to the bar.

"I could hear the music upstairs. It drew me to you." He paused. "I'm totally in awe of you," he murmured, pleased to see a hint of dusky rose color her cheeks.

"Thank you," she said in a breathy voice.

For a moment they held one another's gaze.

"Samantha," Erica said, rushing up to them and kissing Samantha on the cheek. "You were wonderful!" In her excitement she kissed Blake's cheek, too. "Isn't she wonderful, Blake?"

For a split second he froze at Erica's friendliness, but then he found himself relenting toward her even more. Anyone who liked Samantha so much deserved a little more consideration.

He gave his half sister his first ever warm smile. "Yes, she's pretty wonderful."

Erica seemed a little taken aback at his friendliness, but her self-possession soon returned as she spoke to Samantha. "The minute you started playing this afternoon, I knew you were good."

Samantha laughed as she looked from one to the other. "Do either of you have an ear for music?"

"We know a class act when we see it," Erica said, then winked at her half brother. "Don't you agree, Blake?"

Blake nodded, his gaze returning to Samantha and resting there. "I couldn't agree more," he said, as everything inside him went still.

Samantha was class all the way.

Just then, the real guest of honor and her husband came up to thank Samantha for playing so beautifully. Then Anne asked Samantha if she'd play her a special piece of classical music.

And as Blake watched Samantha start to play the piano again, he realized this woman could be destined for better things than being his assistant. He wasn't an expert at piano playing by any means, but he knew when something sounded good. It hit home then that he had no right to keep her here and hold her back from what could be her true vocation. He really did have to let her go. Somewhere at the back of his mind he'd still believed she wouldn't leave. Now he knew different.

"You're amazingly good at playing the piano," he said later, once they were inside Pine Lodge and alone together.

She sent him an amused glance as she took off her coat. "Don't start that again."

He frowned as he took off his own coat and hung it on the rack. "I don't understand why you didn't take your music further. I'm sure you could be a world-class pianist."

She lifted her shoulders in a shrug. "I'm an average pianist. I know my limitations."

He'd been raised to push himself to the limit. "Aren't you putting those limitations on yourself?"

She shook her head. "No, I don't think I am. There are lots of mildly talented people who don't take it all the way. It doesn't mean they're wasting their lives. They can use it in other ways. Some people teach. Some people play for themselves. Others play at parties," she said, her lips curving wryly.

"But—"

She put her hand against his chest. "I don't have the passion for it, Blake. Really, I don't. I like to play occasionally but that's all."

He finally understood what she was saying, but the world had better look out if she ever decided to further her talent.

He felt her palm still against his chest. "What *do* you have a passion for?" he said huskily, bringing it back to the two of them as much as he could. That's what he would focus on from now on. Them and only them.

She rubbed herself against him, seeming to delight in making him aware of her. "Right now? You."

By the time they reached the bedroom they were both naked. After they made love, he pulled her into his arms and let her sleep, but listening to her soft breathing, he admitted to himself that never before had he felt as comfortable after making love to a woman as he did right then. This woman felt right at home in his arms.

And he wasn't sure he should like the feeling.

Ten

One advantage of sleeping with the boss was that she didn't have to jump out of bed and hurry to get to work, Samantha thought lazily, after she woke late the next morning and lay in Blake's arms. He was still asleep.

Then he moved a little and she tilted her head back to look up at him. "You're awake?" she said unnecessarily.

He opened his eyes. "I have been for a while."

That surprised her. Usually the minute he woke up he made love to her.

"Is something wrong?"

"No," he said, but she felt his chest muscles tighten beneath her.

She saw that he had a closed look about him. Something must be on his mind, though she didn't know what. He'd been fine when they'd made love last night. Now he seemed…distant.

She could only think something had occurred to him during the night and upset him. For some reason a wall had been erected between them now. Then she remembered how Erica and Christian had seen him kiss her on the forehead before the party. It hadn't been a passionate kiss but it was clearly more than friendship. So perhaps Blake minded that his family knew about them now? As far as she could tell, it was the only thing that had changed overnight.

"Erica and Christian probably realize we're lovers now," she said, testing the waters.

"They'd be stupid if they didn't." It wasn't said nastily, but it still made her wonder.

She tilted her head back a little. "You don't mind?" He'd looked more at ease with Erica last night. He'd actually seemed to like his half sister.

"Why should I?"

"True." She swallowed. "I'm leaving soon so it doesn't matter anyway, does it?" she said, trying to get a reaction out of him. *Any* reaction. One that didn't lock her out.

There was nothing.

Feeling disheartened, she pushed herself out of bed and hurried to the shower, a tightness in her throat. Their remaining time together was so short. She didn't want to spend it like this.

No sooner had she stepped under the spray than he opened the sliding doors. "What's the matter?" he said, frowning at her.

She thanked goodness the water streaming over her head hid any tears that threatened. "Nothing."

His look said he didn't believe her as he stepped inside the cubicle and joined her. He didn't say a word, and he had a fixed look about him as he soaped them both up and then made love to her with an urgency that startled her. By the end of it she was none the wiser, but at least she knew he still wanted her.

Her heart twisted inside her then. As much as it was a compliment to her, was he still refusing to accept that she was leaving? If so, he was only making it harder for himself. They *both* had to accept it, she thought, her heart aching at the thought.

She managed a blank face as they went to the manor for breakfast. It was either that or cry, and she couldn't allow herself that luxury.

As they entered the lobby, a woman practically jumped out at them. "Blake Jarrod!" she exclaimed, in a you-are-a-naughty-boy tone. "You didn't tell me you owned this hotel." Her gaze slid to Samantha, "Or that your assistant was the piano player."

Blake put on a practiced smile but Samantha could tell he didn't like the woman. "It's Clarice, isn't it?" he said, making it clear he wasn't interested. "This is my assistant *and* piano player," he mocked, "Samantha."

Samantha inclined her head and the woman gave her a cool smile. "I'm Clarice Richardson. Mrs. Clarice Richardson, but I'm *divorced*." Her gaze slid to Blake, instantly dismissing Samantha. "I was wondering, Blake. How would you like to have that drink tonight?"

Blake shook his head. "Can't do, I'm afraid. I have a prior commitment tonight."

"Then how about a cup of coffee now?" the woman said, not giving up. "I have a free morning. In fact, I'm free for the whole day. I'm looking for someone to take me for a drive to Independence Pass."

"Sorry, but I have to get to work."

Clarice gave a tinkle of a laugh that grated on Samantha's nerves. "But you're the boss."

"Which is exactly why I'd better do some work," he said smoothly, then put his hand under Samantha's elbow. "If you'll excuse us."

"Oh. Of course," Clarice said, but Samantha saw her mouth purse with irritation as they walked away.

Then she realized Blake was walking her to the elevator instead of the eatery. "Aren't we having breakfast?"

"We'll get something sent up."

She gave a soft laugh. "Don't tell me you're scared of Mrs. Richardson?"

He shot her a wry look that said he wasn't scared of anyone. "No, but I don't want to deal with her."

"She's persistent, that's for sure." Samantha paused, thinking about something as they stepped inside the elevator and the doors shut. "So you're going out tonight?" She didn't want to sound demanding like Clarice, but as his lover she hoped *she* had a temporary claim on his time right now.

"No, I'm staying home. *You're* my prior commitment."

"I am?" Relief went through her.

He slipped his hand around her waist and pulled her hip against his. "And if I go for a drive to Independence Pass it will be with only one lady."

"Melissa?" she teased.

"You." He kissed her quickly on the mouth just as the doors started to open.

They met Erica as they stepped out of the elevator and into the corridor. She came hurrying forward with a big smile on her face. "Samantha, I want to thank you once again for the fabulous job you did last night."

Samantha returned the smile. "You're very welcome, Erica. I enjoyed it."

Erica considered her. "You know, I've already had a call from the president of the local music school. They heard about you and want to meet with you," she said enthusiastically, making Samantha's heart sink. "They have this huge summer festival where nearly a thousand students and faculty come together from far and wide. There's orchestral concerts and chamber music and—"

Samantha had to stop her there. "I'm sorry, Erica. It wouldn't be any use. I'm leaving soon." She felt Blake stiffen beside her.

Erica's eyes widened. "Oh, I thought—"

Blake muttered something about starting work and stalked off. For a moment Samantha wondered if he was still thinking about her not taking her piano playing seriously, but she soon dismissed it. This wasn't about her not playing the piano. It was about her leaving.

Erica looked at her and winced. "Sorry if I said something out of place."

Samantha tried to smile. "You didn't." She started to follow him. "But I'd better get to work."

Blake was closing his door behind him as she entered her office, and Samantha's heart sank. So. They were back to that again. Talk about a temperamental boss!

Shortly after, he buzzed her for coffee. When she took it into him he seemed okay if a little preoccupied, and she realized she was reading more into this than she should. He had the resort issues to concentrate on and was trying to get the feel for it, that's all. Besides, just because she was now his lover, it shouldn't upgrade her status from his assistant. On the contrary, here at work she'd be upset if it did.

Around eleven he opened his door and strode through her office, scowling. "I'll be with Trevor in his office." He left before she could make any acknowledgement.

Getting to her feet, she went to empty Blake's out tray. There were some letters he'd signed and...all at once she noticed he'd been reading through the files with the résumés. Her heart dropped. That file had sat on his desk untouched all day yesterday, but now he must be thinking ahead.

She should be pleased he wouldn't be left without an assistant, but she could only feel upset. And that was made worse as she went back to her desk and opened the agenda for tomorrow's meeting and saw one of the items was to discuss her replacement.

Oh, God.

So she didn't need Clarice to make a sudden appearance in her office about fifteen minutes later. "Mrs. Richardson, how did you get up here?" she asked, as the woman came toward her desk. A card key was needed for both the private elevator and the back stairs.

"I told one of the staff that I urgently needed to see the person in charge. And I do."

After seeing how Clarice had operated downstairs with Blake, the other woman would have refused to take no for an answer. More than likely she'd even given the staff member a monetary "donation."

Samantha frowned. She would deal with the security breach later. "This is a private area. You shouldn't be here at all. If you needed anything, you should ask at the front desk."

The woman sent her a haughty look. "I'd prefer to deal with Blake, Miss…"

"Thompson." Samantha recognized being put in her place. "Blake's not here at the moment," she said his name deliberately, "but I can pass on a message when he gets back. Now let me walk you to the elevator."

Clarice looked disappointed. Then, "I'll give you my room number." She picked up a sticky-note pad from the desk and wrote on it. "You'll make sure you tell him Clarice called, won't you?" she said, tearing off the slip of paper and handing it to Samantha.

"Of course."

Clarice went to turn away then spun back. "Tell him that I have a proposition for him," she said in a breathless voice.

"Fine." There was nothing to worry about with Blake, but it annoyed Samantha to have to deal with another woman who threw herself at him. There had been so many of them over the years. Clarice was very attractive, but so were the other women who had chased Blake.

Samantha stayed at her desk and waited for Blake to return for lunch. Knowing she was being contrary, she was still upset that he was looking at replacing her, and now she just wanted to spend more time with him. But he didn't return until after lunch, and she spent a quiet lunch break by herself.

"There's a plate of sandwiches on your desk," she said when he walked back through to his office.

"I ate lunch with Trevor."

It would have been nice to be told, she decided, then admitted to herself that as her boss, Blake didn't owe her his time.

She followed him into his office. "Here are your

messages. You'll see there's one from Mrs. Richardson."
When his face remained blank, she said, "Clarice."

He let out a heavy sigh. "What does she want?"

"For you to call her. She delivered it in person."

He scowled. "How did she get up here?"

Samantha told him. "I've passed on my concern to
the front desk. They're going to look into it."

He nodded. "Good."

"By the way, Clarice left her room number for you to
call her back. She says to tell you she has a proposition
for you."

"A proposition?" He grimaced. "I bet she does."

Samantha picked up the plate of sandwiches and put
them in the refrigerator near her desk, feeling better
that Clarice hadn't fooled him. Not that she expected he
wouldn't see through it all. He knew more about women
than she did herself.

It was fairly quiet for the next two hours as Blake
returned messages and she typed up some reports. Then,
he came out carrying his coat. "I have to go into town
for a meeting. It'll take a few hours."

She almost asked if she could go with him, then
stopped. Her place as his assistant was here.

Suddenly he came over and kissed her hard. "I'll see
you later at the lodge. We can go out for dinner if you
like."

She shook her head, pleased. "No, let's eat in. I'll get
something from the hotel kitchen on the way home."

His eyes flickered, and she suspected he'd noticed
her mention of the word *home*. "Okay." He left.

Not long after that, Samantha decided to go down
to the kitchen to see about tonight's dinner. She took
the plate of sandwiches down to the front desk, as one

of the staff might appreciate them for later, rather than throwing them in the trash.

She was walking through the lobby toward the front desk when out of the corner of her eye she happened to glance over at the bar. Her heart stuttered. Blake and Clarice were sitting in there having a drink. Both of them were focused on each other, though she noted Clarice was leaning toward him and doing the talking, more with her cleavage than not. Was this where the other woman offered her "proposition?"

So much for his appointment in town, Samantha thought, not sure what she was doing as she spun around and headed back to her office, giving herself time to adjust to what she'd seen. She had to put this into perspective.

Okay, so there was probably nothing to it, but she just didn't like that Blake was telling her one thing, then doing another. And wasn't he getting Clarice's hopes up even by sitting with the woman? Then again, he was a free man and once *she* left Aspen he would get lonely. The other woman was certainly beautiful.

Samantha threw the sandwiches in the trash, unable to face going back downstairs again. Instead, she phoned the kitchen and ordered two meals for dinner, though she wasn't sure she would feel hungry.

Blake seemed lost in thought when he returned to the lodge that evening, so Samantha didn't mention it straightaway. Besides, she didn't want to sound like a harping wife.

She managed to wait until they had almost finished dinner before saying offhand, "By the way, Blake. Next time you *don't* plan on having a drink with Mrs. Richardson, don't do it in the bar."

His eyes narrowed. "What does that mean?" he said coolly, thankfully not looking the least bit guilty.

"I saw you with her," she said, still keeping her voice casual.

He frowned. "So?"

She lifted one shoulder. "I just thought it odd that you weren't 'free' to spend time with her...and then you were."

He had an arrested expression, before a look of male satisfaction crossed his face. "You sound jealous."

She tried not to look flustered. If he thought she was jealous then he might realize she was more emotionally involved with him than she was letting on. "It's not in my nature to be jealous," she lied, quickly disabusing him of that.

His eyes sharpened. "So you don't mind if I go out with other women, then?"

"While I'm here in Aspen, I *do* mind," she said, seeing his jaw tense. "I think a person should show respect for their lover, don't you?"

There was a moment's pause before he gave a brief nod. "I totally agree, Samantha. Lovers should be true to each other."

"Thank you."

He broke eye contact and took a sip of his wine. "Anyway, you have nothing to worry about with Clarice. She waylaid me as I was leaving for my meeting in town and I felt I had to hear her out. Her proposition is a business one. She owns a chain of high-end boutiques and she wanted to know if she can put one here at Jarrod Ridge."

Samantha digested the information. Now she felt foolish for jumping to conclusions about Clarice.

Yet not.

"It's purely about business," Blake assured her. "I'm going to speak to the family about it at tomorrow morning's meeting."

Her heart constricted at the thought of what else was on tomorrow's agenda—the résumés for her replacement. She noted he didn't mention that right now.

Trying not to think about it, she concentrated on what the other woman's proposition would mean. "Clarice will be here in Aspen a lot, then." And *she* wouldn't be. Clarice would have a clear field with Blake.

He frowned. "I'm not sure. I'd say while it's being set up, she'll visit on and off from L.A." His eyes caught hers. "Why?"

She schooled her features. "No reason. I was merely thinking out loud." She planted on a smile. "And of course I won't be here anyway, so it doesn't concern me."

His eyes turned somewhat hostile. "That's right. What do you care anyway?"

"Exactly," she agreed, her heart breaking. She stood up. "I'll get dessert." She hurried out of the room, aware that he still didn't understand why she had to leave and thanking God he didn't. She took comfort knowing he had no idea she loved him.

Unfortunately the marvelous chocolate concoction in the refrigerator wouldn't lessen her inner pain. She doubted anything ever would.

"…And now that the Food and Wine Gala is completely out of the way for this year," Blake said the next morning, looking down the boardroom table at his siblings, "let's move on to the next thing on the agenda.

Gavin, can you give everyone an update on the bungalow project."

Blake already knew the details of the project, so he found his mind straying back to Samantha. Last night at dinner he'd actually been pleased that she might be jealous of Clarice. Never before had he wanted a woman to feel jealousy over him. Samantha had soon disabused him of that, but appeared to deliberately bring up the fact that she was leaving soon just to goad him. And he'd retaliated by lashing out with an I-don't-care attitude.

Only trouble was…he *did* care. And he couldn't shake that feeling. It kept hitting him in the face no matter where he turned. She didn't seem to realize how much he was going to miss her. If she did, would she still leave? He'd already made it clear he didn't want her to go. Hell, she should be here at his side right now taking notes. Instead, he deliberately told her not to bother attending the meeting today. Not when *she* was on the agenda.

"Blake, I've finished," he heard Gavin say.

He blinked and saw the others staring at him. He had to get back to business. "Right. The next item on the agenda is mainly for you, Trevor. One of the wealthy guests has approached me about opening a boutique here at the lodge." He explained further.

Trevor nodded as he listened. "Sounds good. We could see—"

There was a tap at the door.

Samantha came into the room, looking slightly apologetic. "I'm sorry for the interruption, but Trevor's assistant asked me to give him a message." She walked toward Trevor and passed him a piece of paper. "I ran into Diana downstairs," she said directly to him. "She was on her way up here, so I said I'd hand it to you and save her coming up." Then she gave a general smile and turned to leave the room.

Blake watched her walk away with a slight sway to her hips that emphasized the soft lines of her body, but as she closed the door behind her, he heard Trevor mildly curse.

"What's the matter, Trev?" Guy was the first to ask.

Trevor looked at the note and shook his head. "I don't know what's going on. It's some woman called Haylie Smith. She left a message the other day saying it's important she speak with me but that it's private and she won't discuss it with anyone else. I've never even heard of her."

"Maybe she's got a crush on you?" Gavin mocked.

Trevor shot his brother a look that wasn't amused. "I don't mind a novel approach but this is getting ridiculous."

"Perhaps you should call her back," Melissa suggested.

Trevor shook his head. "No, if it was that important she could leave a message as to why." He grimaced. "I'll have to let Diana know not to interrupt my meetings in future."

"Maybe you should get a tap on your phone," Christian said, ever the lawyer.

Erica looked at her fiancé. "Darling, the woman's only left two messages. Hardly enough reason to put a stalking charge on her."

"Hey, who said anything about a stalker?" Trevor choked.

"I think—" Melissa began.

"People, can we focus here," Blake cut across her. "We have other matters at hand."

A few seconds ticked by.

Then Trevor nodded. "Yes, of course." His forehead creased as he thought. "Now, where was I? Right. I think we can give this Mrs. Richardson a short-term lease and see how it goes. I'm sure she won't want a long-term lease anyway."

Blake agreed. "Good idea. Perhaps you'd like to check out her business practices and financial situation before we decide anything further."

"Sure."

Blake turned to Melissa. "How's the spa going, Melissa?"

Melissa launched into a brief report.

"And now we need to discuss plans for the upcoming ski season." Blake looked at his half sister. "Erica, I believe you were going to prepare a report on how the Christmas bookings and the hiring of staff are going."

Erica inclined her head, looking very efficient. "Yes, Blake, that's right. I've drawn up a presentation, so if you'll all just look at the screen…"

Blake glanced at the screen, immediately impressed by Erica's attention to detail, and he couldn't help but surreptitiously glance at Christian sitting down the table on his right. The other man was looking at Erica with pride and admiration. But Blake saw something in the other man's features that reminded him of how *he* felt whenever he looked at Samantha.

Samantha.

Something twisted inside him. In less than ten days she would return to Vegas to wrap up everything. Then in another two weeks she would be out of his life and gone for good. He swallowed hard. There was nothing good about her going, he decided, dropping his gaze to the paperwork in front of him in case the others saw his thoughts.

The next agenda item jumped out at him.

Samantha's replacement.

Dammit, he had to do this. It was time to bring to the table a list of suitable applications for her position. It was only fair he keep his family up-to-date. After all, the new applicant would be mainly working out of here now and he wanted everyone to—

Just then there was another tap at the door and Samantha stuck her head around it, then entered the room farther. "I'm sorry, Blake, but there's an urgent message here for you from Mrs. Richardson. She wants you to call her back as soon as you can. It's to do with her boutique."

Here was the woman who was leaving him. The woman who could so easily walk away from what they had. Resentment rose in his chest and up his throat. He was tying himself up in knots for her and she was standing there looking so damn poised and polite.

And so damn beautiful.

Something snapped inside him right then. "I'm sure whatever Mrs. Richardson has to say can wait. Please keep any other messages for us until we finish this meeting," he dismissed, hearing himself talk in that harsh tone like he was listening to someone else talk to her.

Samantha flinched, then went to leave but turned back and squared her shoulders, a rebuke in her eyes. "Of course, Mr. Jarrod," she said primly and left the room with quiet dignity.

The door closed behind her.

All eyes were turned on him.

"I don't think there was any need for that, Blake," Guy said quietly.

Blake felt bad. If she hadn't come in at that moment then he wouldn't have verbally attacked her. It had been a reaction to her leaving him, not a reaction to *her*.

He looked at them. They were staring back at him with reproachful eyes that reminded him of Samantha. His mouth tightened. "I know, I know. I'll apologize later." He put thoughts of that to the side. "Now. Speaking of Samantha, as you know she's leaving. I'm looking at other applicants and I think one of them will be eminently suitable to replace her."

Guy arched a brow. "Can anyone replace her?"

"Guy," Blake growled.

"Blake," Melissa began, "don't you think—"

"No, Melissa," he said firmly, without being rude, knowing what she was going to say. "All of you listen to me. This is private between Samantha and myself. It's none of your business. Now. Let's talk about finding me a new assistant so that we can end this meeting and get on with other things."

The tension in the air was palpable, but he ignored both it and the looks on their faces. He owed no one any explanation. Hell, what explanation could there be anyway?

Samantha wanted to leave.

Samantha *was* leaving.

And he hated himself for embarrassing her just now.

"I apologize, Samantha."

Samantha had heard him enter the office but she'd

ignored him. Now she lifted her head to find Blake standing in front of her desk. Anger and hurt rioted inside her. She had to keep busy.

She rose to her feet and went to put some papers in the filing cabinet. "I'm glad I'm leaving now."

"Don't be like that."

She spun around. "Like what, Blake? Standing up for myself?"

His eyes clouded over. "Look, I know I embarrassed you in front of the family. I shouldn't have done that. I'm sorry."

She lifted her chin. "I was only doing my job. I'm not a novice at this. The woman said it was urgent, and seeing that her proposal was on the agenda for the meeting, I assumed you'd want to know any important developments."

"I know. And you're right. You did the right thing." His expression turned sincere. "You may not believe this, but the reason I snapped was because of you. I was angry because I had to bring up mention of your replacement. I don't want a replacement. I want *you*."

Her heart skipped a beat and she began to soften. She didn't doubt him. She never doubted what he said. If he said something, he meant it. He wasn't manipulating her. He'd accepted that she was leaving and he had nothing to lose by being honest. Why fight with him when time was so precious between them?

She thawed. "Oh, Blake."

He came toward her and slipped his arms around her waist. "Forgive me for being a pig? The others know I feel bad. Their sympathy was all on your side, believe me."

"Let's forget it." But it was nice to know his family had stuck up for her, especially against their big brother.

He lifted his hand and stroked her cheek. "Are you sure you don't want to change your mind about leaving? It would be good between us."

She drew a painful breath. "No, I can't." He wanted short-term. She wanted forever. And he wasn't a forever type of guy.

His eyes shadowed with regret and he lowered his head and kissed her. She opened her mouth to him, knowing this was the only way she could let him inside herself.

The telephone rang just then and they both ignored it.

It stopped, then rang again.

She pulled back. "I should get that," she said, and Blake nodded with a grimace.

It was Clarice.

Samantha looked at Blake as she listened. Then, "Yes, I passed the message on, Mrs. Richardson."

Blake's mouth tightened and he held his hand out for the phone. "What's the problem, Clarice?" he said, after she handed it to him. There was a pause as he listened. "Look, I'm pretty busy right now." He winked at Samantha and her heart soared with love.

Another pause.

"It was discussed at a meeting this morning. My brother, Trevor, is going to work with you on this." He listened. "Yes. Fine." He hung up, shook his head at it, then kissed Samantha quickly. "I need to go see Trevor and fill him in before Clarice gets to him. Unfortunately I'm not sure he knows what he's coming up against with that woman."

Samantha considered him. "You really worry about your brothers and sisters, don't you?"

"Yes, I suppose I do."

She went up on her toes and kissed him briefly. He looked a little surprised as he turned and left the office. He was a good brother, she decided, her heart beating with love for him.

And a good man.

Eleven

Just before lunch, Melissa popped into the office as Blake was discussing a letter with Samantha. "I've booked you in for a spa treatment with me at four, Samantha. You need some major pampering."

Samantha blinked. "Oh, but—"

"No arguments. I don't give many massages these days but I've decided to give you one." Melissa smiled slyly at her big brother. "Anyway it's Blake's treat."

Blake lifted his brows. "What is it with my sisters bullying me?" Then he smiled at Samantha. "Keep the appointment."

"Okay, thanks." Samantha smiled at Melissa. "And thank you, too, Melissa."

"You're very welcome. See you at four." Melissa started to leave then stopped to consider her big brother. "It would do you good to have one, too, Blake." Her face lit with mischief. "You could share with Samantha. I'll even throw in a bottle of chilled champagne and some chocolate truffles. It's quite decadent."

"Not right now, thanks. I've got a lot to do."

"And that's exactly why you *should* have a massage."

"Soon."

"I'll keep you to that."

After she left, Samantha looked at Blake. "I wish you could come with me."

Heat lurked in the back of his eyes. "So do I, but I've got that meeting in town this afternoon."

His look warmed her through as she tilted her head. "You don't realize, do you?"

"What?"

"That you said *sisters* before."

Not *sister* and *half sister*.

Sisters.

Something flickered across his face, then he shrugged. "Yeah, well, don't make a big deal out of it." He went back into his office and Samantha went back to work, but she felt he'd made a big step in his relationship with his family and she was pleased for them all.

At four, Samantha walked over to the Tranquility Spa. Just stepping into a place that exemplified sophistication and sheer indulgence in a mountain setting relaxed her. It was gorgeous.

Melissa was waiting for her and led her to one of the treatment rooms that had serene music playing in the background. "I'll leave you to take off your clothes. Then slide under that sheet there and lie facedown on the bed. It's heated. I'll be back in a minute."

Samantha did as suggested and five minutes later, Melissa came back. "Good. Now I think a gentle massage should do the trick." There was the sound of her moving about. "Hmm, I'll have to be careful with your head. How is it, by the way?"

Samantha appreciated that Melissa remembered her injury. "Much better, thanks. It's healing well."

"I'm pleased. It could have been so much worse." Melissa started to rub oil on Samantha's back. "I hear Blake was quite upset about it."

"He blamed himself because he insisted I go with him for a drive."

"My brother's deep at times."

"I know." Samantha groaned as Melissa began long strokes to help soften the muscles.

"Am I hurting you?"

"No, not at all. It's exquisite."

Melissa laughed. "There's nothing like a massage." She continued working wonders, finding the right spots with unerring accuracy. Then, "Blake was pretty hard on you in the conference room today."

Samantha was glad she was lying on the bed with her face turned to the other side. "He apologized later."

"I knew he would. He's a man who knows when he's in the wrong."

"A rare boss," Samantha said, trying to make light of it.

"And a rare man."

"Right on both counts," Samantha just had to agree, then gave a little moan of pleasure as the massaging reached the base of her neck. She hadn't realized how badly she needed this.

Conversation ceased for a bit, before Melissa said, "I think Blake might be getting used to Erica."

Samantha wasn't surprised by the comment. "So you noticed that he said *sisters,* did you?"

"Oh, yeah."

"Erica's really nice."

"I love her already." Genuine warmth filled Melissa's voice. "It's like we're full sisters, not half sisters. We connected together right from the start."

"You've been really great at welcoming her into the family, Melissa. Erica must have appreciated that, especially when it came to the cool attitudes of her brothers."

"Those guys are so stubborn at times, and now look at them. They'll protect her to the death. I suspect even Blake would, too."

Back to Blake.

It always came back to Blake.

Time to change the subject. "So how is business doing at the spa?"

"Quiet right now, but next month it'll start picking up. And in December we'll be run off our feet. Of course, Shane worries about me and the baby, so I've promised him I'll put on extra staff."

"I can understand that."

There was a tiny pause. "This baby means so much to us," she said, with a little catch in her voice that tugged at Samantha's heartstrings.

"Pregnancy suits you. You're glowing."

Melissa cleared her throat. "Thanks. I can highly recommend it." All at once there was a slight change in the air. "What about you, Samantha? Do you plan on having children one day?"

Samantha swallowed the despair in her throat at the thought of having Blake's baby. She forced herself to sound natural. "Yes, I'd love to. But only when the time is right and with the right man."

There was no immediate reply. Then, "Forgive me for saying this, but isn't Blake the right man for you? Wouldn't you like to have his baby?"

Samantha's heart constricted as she was forced to face something she hadn't dared let herself think about now that she knew she loved Blake. This was dangerous territory for her. Loving him like she did and having his baby would be so absolutely wonderful, but knowing it was never going to happen was like a knife through her heart.

She swallowed hard again, then somehow said calmly, "You should know your brother by now, Melissa. Blake isn't into commitment, and having a baby would be a *huge* commitment."

Besides, Blake was already a father figure to his brothers and sisters, and he was already married to his job. There wasn't room for her, even if he actually *wanted* her to be a part of it all.

"Is that why you're leaving?"

She didn't hesitate. She couldn't afford to. "No. I'm leaving because it's the best thing for me."

There was a short silence, then, "I see."

Much to Samantha's relief, Melissa changed the subject and they talked about more desultory things on and off until the massage was over.

"Now," Melissa finally said, after she'd tidied up. "How do you feel?"

"Like I'm about to slither off the bed."

Melissa laughed. "That's what we aim for. Right, I'm going to leave you to get dressed. Take your time and don't rush. And make sure you drink lots of water for the next couple of hours. The massage releases toxins and if you don't flush them out you'll end up with a toxic headache."

"That sounds lethal," Samantha joked as she managed to push herself into a sitting position and wrapped the sheet around herself. "Thank you so much for this, Melissa," she said sincerely. "I didn't know how much I needed it. I really do feel wonderful."

Melissa smiled as she headed for the door. "Then I've done my job."

Samantha watched her leave, her smile fading as soon as the door closed, leaving her alone. Her body might feel better, but how did a person continue with a broken heart? Unfortunately no one could fix that.

"How was the massage?"

Samantha closed the front door behind her and saw Blake leaning against the kitchen doorjamb, as if he'd been waiting for her to come home. This was how it would be if she were to stay here with him. Yet how long would it last? Certainly not forever. Eventually things would become awkward between them and he would start to avoid her.

And then she'd know he would no longer want her.

"Wonderful," she said, giving him a smile that somehow felt empty.

"What's the matter?"

She looked at him and her heart felt sore. She couldn't seem to shake herself out of her despondency. "I think I need you to hold me, Blake."

"Why?"

"I just do, okay?"

He pushed himself away from the wall and came toward her, pulling her close. "Is that better?"

She slid her arms around him. "Yes." But a shiver went through her.

His brow wrinkled as he looked down at her. "What's going on with you?"

She drew a breath. "We won't have this for much longer."

He stiffened. "And?"

His reaction told her all she needed to know. "I feel... sad it's coming to an end."

"It's your choice to leave, Samantha."

She kept her face perfectly straight. "I know." He didn't understand and she couldn't say any different. "I want to go to bed, Blake. Let's make love until the sun comes up."

It could have sounded silly but he didn't smile and she was glad about that. It was as if he knew this meant a lot to her. And regardless of him avoiding any type of commitment, she hoped it would mean a lot to him, too.

In his bedroom she kept her eyes closed as she made love to him with everything in her heart. The thought of leaving him...of never having his child...of not sharing his life forever...was utmost in her mind. She'd never before felt such profound depth of emotion and she cried softly afterward. It would be so much worse once she left Blake for good.

Blake carefully eased out of bed the next morning just before sunrise, drew on his pajama pants and robe and left Samantha to sleep as he went downstairs to make himself some coffee. He felt restless, with a hard knot in his gut that he couldn't shake. Samantha had cried last night after they'd made love. She hadn't done that before. And it made him wonder. It was obvious she had strong feelings for him and he was certain now those feelings were the reason for her leaving. She hadn't said the words out loud, but he'd felt it every time she touched him and in her cry of release. Could she *love* him?

He couldn't love her back.

Hell, he should have seen this coming. *He* was the experienced one after all. Okay, so he'd invested more of himself in this relationship than he'd planned, but falling in love with Samantha, or any woman, wasn't on his agenda. It never had been and never would be. He'd never allow any person that much control over him.

Never.

So where did they go from there? Exactly nowhere. She'd leave and he'd let her go. End of story. There would be no happy ending for them. He couldn't give her that. He wished to heaven he could. He hated hurting her like this, especially knowing her last boyfriend had rejected her, too. She must feel so totally unwanted. Cast-off. Discarded and abandoned. God, how he hated to do this to her. It really pained him to do this. He shuddered, then reminded himself. He *had* warned her. And now that it came down to the crunch *she* had to be responsible for her own reactions.

Just then, the security light came on over the back decking and he saw a figure coming up the steps. The man was wrapped up to ward off the pre-sunrise chill, but he'd know that gait anywhere.

He opened the back door just as Gavin reached for the handle. "I see you smelled the coffee."

His brother smiled as he stepped inside the kitchen. "Sure did."

Blake went to get another mug down from the cupboard. "What are you doing out and about so early?"

Gavin began taking off his thick gloves. "I was going for a walk to clear my head and saw the light on."

Blake frowned a little as he poured coffee into the mugs. "Anything in particular bothering you?"

"Not really."

He handed one of the mugs to his brother. "Is the bungalow project worrying you?"

"Not at all." Gavin shrugged. "I guess it just feels strange being back home again. It hits me most at this time of the morning, and that means I usually need to get some fresh air."

Blake understood. "I know what you mean."

Gavin shot him a curious look. "I'm surprised. Don't you have a lovely lady warming your bed, helping keep those thoughts at bay?"

Blake kept his face blank. "Do I?"

Gavin shook his head. "You always were the same about never sharing your feelings with anyone."

Blake's lips twisted. "Yeah, like *you* do?"

"All I can say is that you must be losing your touch where Samantha is concerned."

"Why?" He knew he shouldn't bite, but Samantha was so much on his mind this morning.

"I thought for sure you wouldn't be dumb enough to let her go."

Blake immediately went on the defensive. "Why would I want her to stay?"

"You need to ask?" Gavin shook his head. "How about she's excellent at her job, she's a looker and a nice person to boot, and as much as I hate to say it, she's damn good for you, that's why. You'll never find an assistant who anticipates your needs the way she does."

Blake dropped his gaze to the mug of coffee in his hands. What Gavin said was true, except the bit about Samantha being good for him. He didn't need any woman to make him feel good.

And he didn't like his brother getting too close and figuring out something that didn't need figuring out. Certainly he didn't want his brother figuring out that Samantha was in love with *him,* and that he couldn't return her love. He had to protect her. He didn't want anyone talking about her even after she left here. He owed her that much.

"Yeah, she's more than competent at her job and she's beautiful, too, but so are many other women. As for being good for me...yeah, we've had some fun while it lasted but it's coming to an end now and I'm more than happy with that."

Gavin sent him a challenging look. "So you feel nothing more for her?"

"No," he lied, feeling like Judas.

"I'm sorry to hear that," Gavin said slowly.

Suddenly a figure stepped into the doorway. "Don't be, Gavin," Samantha said quietly, hurt in her lovely eyes but dignity in her face. "I'm not."

Blake's heart cramped. "Samantha, I—"

"No need to explain, Blake. I shouldn't have eaves-dropped but I'm glad I did. I would never have guessed you felt so little for me," she said, a catch to her voice.

He took a step toward her. "Samantha—"

She put up her hand. "No, Blake. You've said more

than enough." She turned and hurried away so fast all he saw was her shadow.

Shit!

Gavin lifted a brow. "Seems to me she might mean more to you than you think."

Blake tried to focus. "No, you're wrong."

Gavin stared hard, then put his mug down on the bench. "I'll leave you two to sort things out."

Blake gave a jerky nod as his brother headed for the back door and left him to it. He stood there in the kitchen for a minute as regret washed over him before he took the steps to follow her. He'd do his best to mend this damage as much as possible, but if he were to be honest, things between him and Samantha really couldn't be fixed. It was probably best this had come to a head.

Samantha could barely see as she fled up the staircase for the sanctuary of her room. After waking up, she'd gone downstairs in her nightshirt looking for Blake, surprised to hear Gavin's voice and never dreaming they were discussing *her*.

Oh, God. She couldn't stay in Aspen any longer. Not now. This was it. She was leaving as soon as possible, come hell or high water.

She grabbed her suitcases out of the wardrobe and threw them on the bed. She'd always been neat and tidy and fast at packing, but who cared anyway, she decided, swallowing a sob. All she wanted was to throw everything in her bags and get to the airport. She was going home to Pasadena where she would lick her wounds. Beyond that she couldn't think.

"Samantha?" Blake's voice came gently from the doorway.

Refusing to let him see her cry, she blinked back her tears as she carried her sweaters over to one of the suitcases.

"Samantha, stop. We need to talk."

She looked at him but continued what she was doing. "No. I'm leaving. It's time for me to get out of your hair."

And out of your life.

He swore low. "I'm sorry."

She dumped her clothes into the case. "You're only sorry that I overheard you," she said tightly, then took a shuddering breath as humiliation and hurt swelled inside her. "You made it sound so…cheap. You made *me* sound cheap. As if I don't matter."

"You *do* matter," he said, looking pained, but she knew better.

"Just not to you, right?" she derided, despair wrapping around her heart and not letting go.

"I didn't mean to speak like that about you. I just didn't want Gavin to know what was going on between us."

She snorted. "Of course. How silly of me? We can't have the great Blake Jarrod show any feelings now, can we? Not to his family and not to me." It was never about his feelings anyway, and that was the hardest part to take. She'd dared hope he might at least have a high opinion of her. "Your words show me that you never even respected me as a person, Blake. And certainly not as your lover."

His face blanched. "Don't say that," he growled. "I respect you. There's no one I respect more."

"It didn't sound like that to me back there." All at once she took a shuddering breath and admitted that she couldn't blame him for everything. "But I'm doing you a disservice. You made me no promises, I'll allow you that. You tried to warn me not to get involved with you."

His gaze sharpened. "And did you?"

What did she have to lose now? "Of course I did. I..." She couldn't say she loved him. She just couldn't. That would be too humiliating. "...I thought we had something special."

"We do."

She shook her head. "We *did*. It's over." Suddenly she caught a subtle change in his face—a change that Carl hadn't shown when he'd rejected her. She stilled. Her breath stopped. Did Blake have feelings for her after all? "Unless..." *Dare she ask?* "Can you give me one good reason to stay?"

Silence fell.

She waited. She couldn't say the words but he must know what she was asking. If ever there was a time he might let down his guard...a time when he could allow her into his heart...it would surely be—

His face closed up. "No, I'm sorry. I can't give you a reason to stay."

As hard as it was to pull herself together, she recovered her breath. "That's what I thought."

"Sam—"

A hard laugh escaped then. "Too late to call me that, Blake. Far too late." She held her head up higher. "Now, please leave me to pack in peace. It was good while it lasted but it's over between us now."

He stiffened, withdrawing into himself. "I'm really sorry I hurt you."

She held his gaze. "So am I. And as horrible as this

sounds, I wish I *was* capable of hurting you back." It would at least show she had meant something to him.

Turning away, he stopped and said over his shoulder, "The family jet is at your disposal. It'll take you wherever you want to go."

The words stung her heart. "Thank you."

He strode down the hallway to his suite, going inside and quietly closing the door behind him, shutting her out of his life. For good.

Samantha made herself move. She walked to her door and closed it, then went and sat on the bed and picked up a pillow to muffle her sobs. She figured this time she was entitled to cry.

Twelve

Half an hour later, Blake had showered and dressed and now sat in his office at the Manor, his leather chair turned toward the picture window. An early fall snow that wasn't unusual at this time of year had begun covering the resort, and now a weak sun was shining on the surrounding mountains. Usually at this time he was back at Pine Lodge making love to Samantha. All he could think now was that she was leaving.

God, she'd been so hurt back there. It had pained him to realize how much. And yet he hadn't been able to say the words to get her to stay. He'd known what she wanted, of course. She wanted him to say he loved her, but those words were no longer in his vocabulary. The last time he'd used them had been all those years ago to his mother—just before she died. He'd never said them again to anyone. He'd accepted he never would.

His upbringing—his whole life since—had been about avoiding commitment.

And now Samantha had to accept that, too.

Just then he heard a noise behind him and his chest instantly tightened. She'd come to say her final goodbye.

"What happened with Samantha, Blake?"

Erica.

He twisted his chair around, forcing his brain to work as he looked at the unhappy face of his half sister. Clearly she'd spoken to Gavin not too long ago.

He picked up a pen. "She's packing to leave."

"So you're just going to let her go?"

He gave a shrug. "She wants to go. I can't stop her."

She came closer to the desk, frowning. "What's gone so wrong with you two?"

He shot her a hostile look. "It's none of your business, Erica."

"You're my brother. I'm making it my business."

"Half brother," he corrected.

"I'm so sick of this," she snapped, drawing her petite frame up taller than she was, glaring down at him, standing her ground. "We have the same blood in our veins and that makes me a Jarrod, Blake. You're my brother, like it or lump it."

He stared up at her, a growing admiration rising inside him as he looked at this woman who was related to him, no matter how much he didn't like it. The angle of her chin. The light of battle in her eyes. That stubbornness in her mouth. Oh, yeah. Erica *was* a Jarrod, through and through.

"Blake, for God's sake, when are you going to drop your guard and let people in?"

He tensed. "I don't know what you mean."

"I mean, you won't let a half sister into your life because you think I might let you down like your mother did when she died. And you won't let Samantha into your heart because of the same thing. You're frightened you'll get hurt."

"That's ridiculous," he snapped. Sure, he wasn't willing to get involved with anyone and lay himself open to hurt, but that was only because he couldn't be bothered with the ramifications of it all. He was too busy to introduce any complications in his life.

"Then tell me why you're letting a beautiful woman like Samantha walk away from you?"

"She wants to go."

"No, *you* want her to go and she knows it."

His jaw clenched. "This has got nothing to do with you, Erica."

"Look at yourself, Blake. You're deliberately making it hard for Samantha to stay. You're pushing her away and abandoning her before she can abandon *you*."

He swore. "Just stay out of this."

"Think about it. Your mother died when you were six, so it stands to reason that you would be affected by her death. And what about your father? Donald Jarrod shut up shop with his emotions when his wife died, and the only way he could cope was by focusing on his offspring. He pushed all of you to be the best you could be, and none more than you as eldest."

"Erica…" he warned.

"I suspect he wanted his kids to be fully reliant on themselves. He didn't want any of you to get hurt. Not like *he* got hurt."

"That's enough."

"So you effectively lost not only your mother when you were little, but your father, as well. Is it any wonder you don't want to let anyone get close to you?"

He opened his mouth again....

And then somehow, without warning, her words began to hit him right where it mattered. But still he had to say, "What I want is not to listen to this drivel."

Her eyes said he wasn't fooling her. "People have their breaking point, Blake. Your mother's death was your—I mean, *our* father's breaking point. A person can do silly things in their grief. Everyone reacts differently. Our father turned to my mother, looking for solace. Who's to say you wouldn't do the same thing?"

"I would never want another woman after Samantha," he growled. "Never."

"Do you hear yourself?"

He stiffened and blinked. "What?"

She stood there watching him in silent scrutiny for a moment. "If Samantha died how would *you* feel?"

"Don't say that," he rasped, the thought slicing down through the middle of him.

"You love her, Blake."

His head reeled back. "No."

"Yes. Don't let yourself realize it too late. You may never get a second chance."

He swallowed as something deep inside him lifted up like a shade on a window and he finally admitted what was right there in front of him.

He *did* love Samantha.

And right then, he finally understood the depth of his father's loss. He still didn't understand how Donald Jarrod could have shunned the children who were a legacy of his beloved wife, nor how his father had turned to another woman, but the idea of Samantha dying squeezed his heart so tight he could barely breathe.

He surged to his feet. "I have to go to her."

"Thank God!"

He glanced at his watch. "She may not have left the lodge."

"She's already taken the valet car. I saw her leaving." Erica made a gesture toward the door. "Go. I'll make sure they stop the plane. And hey, take it easy getting to her, okay? We've got our first snow, and she'll want you in one piece."

"I will." He was almost at the door by the time she finished speaking. All at once he stopped, conscious that he had to take a moment more for something else. He returned to Erica to kiss her on the cheek. "Thanks, sis."

She beamed at him. "You're welcome. Just remember you'll have a few brothers and sisters who'll expect your firstborn to be named after them."

He grinned. "That's a lot of names."

"Well, maybe you can have a lot of kids."

He chuckled as warmth filled him at the thought of Samantha carrying his child. But first things first...he wanted only one person right now.

Samantha.

As he raced down to the lobby, he remembered how after their lovemaking the other night he'd felt so at home in her arms. Now he knew it was more than that.

In Samantha's arms he *had* come home.

"Is it going to be much longer, Jayne?" Samantha asked, after she'd boarded the Jarrod private jet and nothing seemed to be happening. They hadn't even taxied out onto the runway yet.

"I'm sorry about this, Ms. Thompson," the stewardess apologized. "It's the weather. There's a storm ahead. We have to sit tight until it passes."

Samantha swiveled her leather chair around on its base a little to glance out the cabin window to the snow-dusted airport. A few weeks ago, before she'd decided to resign, she'd been eagerly looking forward to the first of the snow falling over Jarrod Ridge. Now she had to return to the warm California weather and try not to imagine how magical it would have been here in Blake's arms.

Somehow she faked a small smile back at the other woman. "Okay, thanks, Jayne."

The stewardess smiled, then went to the back of the plane, leaving her alone to stare out the window. She'd done her best to repair her face after her crying session back at the lodge, but the longer she sat here the more likely she might burst into tears.

And if she did that she would be humiliated in front of Jayne. She wanted no one knowing how painful this was for her. Blake knew she'd been hurt, but he really had no idea at the depths of her despair. How could he? He didn't love her. He was going to move on. He'd probably already written her off as a bad debt, she thought with a touch of hysteria.

Oh, God. This was it. She was actually leaving Aspen…leaving Blake for good. Fresh tears were verging in her eyes when there was a sudden flurry of movement near the doorway. She quickly took a shuddering breath and glanced ahead to check what was happening.

Blake!

He stood there looking at her…so dear to her heart. And then he moved toward her through the wide cabin, and her thoughts kicked in. Was he here merely to make sure she left? She dared not think otherwise.

He stopped in front of her seat and looked down at her. "You didn't say goodbye, Samantha."

She moistened her mouth. "I didn't think you wanted me to."

"I didn't," he said, and her heart twisted tight at his honesty. "The fact is…I didn't want you to say goodbye at all. I still don't want you to leave. I want you to stay with me." He pulled her to her feet, looking at her with an emotion in his eyes that almost blinded her. "I love you, Samantha."

She knew in a heartbeat he was telling the truth. "Say that again," she whispered.

"I love you."

She threw her arms around his neck. "Oh, my God! I love you, too, Blake. So very, very much."

He kissed her then and she clung to him, loving him with every ounce of her being, feeling the pounding of his heart in time with hers. Forevermore.

Finally he pulled back, but kept his arms around her. "I love you, Samantha. I love you more than life itself."

She sighed blissfully. "I feel the same."

He gave her a soft kiss. "After we made love last night, I suspected you loved me."

At the time she'd hoped she'd masked her feelings well. "I gave myself away when I cried, didn't I?"

"Yes, I'm afraid you did, darling."

She went all sappy inside at the endearment, so she

could forgive him anything. "Yet you were still going to let me go."

"You can thank Erica that I didn't. She made me see sense about a couple of things."

"Thank you, sweet Erica," she mused out loud.

He smiled, then it faded on his handsome face, making him more serious. "I hope you can forgive me for what I said to Gavin. You were right. I didn't want anyone knowing my feelings for you. I was even hiding them from myself," he added with self-derision. "And I hope you can believe this, but I was trying to protect you. I didn't want them realizing you had feelings for me either." He lifted his shoulders. "Loving someone is a private thing."

She thanked him with her eyes. "I agree, though they probably suspected anyway. And yes, I do forgive you, darling," she said, loving the sound of that on her own lips and seeing his eyes darken. "If you hadn't said what you did to Gavin, then all this may not have been resolved."

He chuckled. "Erica would have made us resolve it, don't you worry about that. My sister is a very determined woman."

Her heart swelled. So he'd let Erica into his heart, too. How wonderful. Now he could be the man he was meant to be with his family.

And with her.

All at once there was so much to talk about. She'd have to tell him about when she'd actually realized she loved him, and she'd have to come clean about trying to make him jealous. He was bound to get a laugh out of that.

"Samantha," he cut across her thoughts. "I insist you

don't give up your music. I want you to contact that person Erica mentioned at the music school as soon as you can."

"Oh, Blake, I'm not giving up anything," she said softly, and ran her fingers along his chin, loving the feel of its masculine texture. "I've got all I ever wanted right here."

His brows drew together. "But—"

She smiled at the worried look in his eyes. "Okay, I'll contact them. Perhaps sometime in the future I'll be able to help out in some minor way, but please believe that playing the piano isn't important in my life. I enjoy it. I might even take some more lessons, or give lessons for that matter, but living here with you, and being part of your family, will be more than enough for me."

He gave her a searching look, then his shoulders relaxed. "While we're being honest…"

Her heart caught. "Yes?"

"I know you feel I'm letting you down in some way, but…"

She swallowed hard. "But?" What wasn't he telling her? Was he actually in love with someone else? Was she his second choice? Perhaps he—

"Forgive me, Samantha, but I don't think I'll ever be able to call you Sam."

It took a moment to sink in. She laughed and lightly punched his chest. "You think that's funny, don't you?"

He put his hands on either side of her face and looked at her lovingly. "You're Samantha to me. *My* Samantha. Do you mind?"

She blinked back silly tears of happiness. "Of course not." Not anymore. "It makes me feel very special."

"You *are* special, my darling." He placed his lips on hers, then, "Let's go to Vegas right now and get married."

She blinked. "Married?" As crazy as it seemed, she hadn't thought that far ahead. She'd been too busy taking in that he loved her. "You really want to marry me, Blake?"

He stroked her cheek. "Yes. I want your kisses for the rest of my life."

She drew his mouth down to hers and kissed him softly. "Here's one to start with."

When the kiss finished, he said, "Speaking of giving, you haven't *given* me my answer. Will you marry me?"

"Is there any doubt?"

"Not really."

"You're a conceited man, Blake Jarrod," she teased.

"And that's a good thing in this situation, right?"

She sent him a rueful glance, then something came to her. "But don't you want to get married in Aspen with your family present?"

"No. I'm an impatient man. I want to marry you now. Today." He scowled. "Unless *you* want a big wedding?" He didn't wait for her to answer. "I suppose I shouldn't cheat you of a wedding with your family."

She shook her head. "No, I don't need my family there. I love them dearly but they'll understand. All they want is for me to be happy."

"I can guarantee that."

"Then a wedding for two will be just perfect, my love," she murmured, a flood of emotion making her voice husky.

Blake lowered his head to place his lips against

hers. Outside the plane more snowflakes fell in a hush, blanketing everything in a fairy-tale setting. And that was appropriate. Their love was, after all, a fairy tale come true.

* * * * *

COMING NEXT MONTH

Available November 9, 2010

#2047 THE MAVERICK PRINCE
Catherine Mann
Man of the Month

#2048 WEDDING HIS TAKEOVER TARGET
Emilie Rose
Dynasties: The Jarrods

#2049 TEXAS TYCOON'S CHRISTMAS FIANCÉE
Sara Orwig
Stetsons & CEOs

#2050 TO TAME A SHEIKH
Olivia Gates
Pride of Zohayd

#2051 THE BILLIONAIRE'S BRIDAL BID
Emily McKay

#2052 HIGH-SOCIETY SEDUCTION
Maxine Sullivan

SDCNM1010

REQUEST YOUR FREE BOOKS!

2 FREE NOVELS
PLUS 2
FREE GIFTS!

Passionate, Powerful, Provocative!

"It's okay. I'm here to help." The voice was as deep as the darkness, but Jenna Dougherty didn't believe the lie. She could do nothing but lie still as hands slid down her arms, felt the rope around her wrists.

"I'm going to use a knife to cut you free, Jenna. Hold still."

The cold blade of a knife pressed close to her head before her gag fell away.

"I—" she started, but her mouth was dry, and she could do nothing but suck in air.

"Shhh. Whatever needs to be said can be said when we're out of here." Nick spoke quietly, his hand gentle on her cheek. There and gone as he sliced through the ropes on her wrists and ankles.

He pulled her upright. "Come on. We may be on borrowed time."

"I can't leave my friend," Jenna rasped out.

"There's no one here. Just us."

"She has to be here." Jenna took a step away.

"There's no one here. Let's go before that changes."

"It's dark. Maybe if we find a light…"

"What did you say?"

"We need to turn on the light. I can't leave until I know that—"

"What can you see, Jenna?"

"Nothing."

"No shadows? No light?"

"No."

"It's broad daylight. There's light spilling in from the window I climbed in through. You can't see it?"

She went cold at his words.

"I can't see anything."

"You've got a nasty bruise on your forehead. Maybe that has something to do with it." His fingers traced the tender flesh on her forehead.

"It doesn't matter *how* it happened. I'm blind!"

Can Nick help Jenna find her friend or will chasing this trail have Jenna running blindly again into danger?

Find out in RUNNING BLIND, available in November 2010 only from Love Inspired Suspense.

SHLISEXP1110